Popcorn, Paris, and Paper Napkins

BRENDA STROUPE

To order additional copies of this book, contact:
Xlibris Corporation
1-888-795-4274
www.Xlibris.com
Orders@Xlibris.com

26504

Contents

Dedication

This book is dedicated to Daniel "Butch" Blackwelder. Without his inspiration, it would still be lying on a shelf half finished, collecting dust.

ACKNOWLEDGMENTS

I would like to thank all of the friends and relatives who believed in this little book and encouraged me throughout the years to have it published. I especially want to thank Brenda Saine for the many weeks she spent typing so many summers ago allowing me to continue writing the book itself. I want to thank Blake Carpenter for the many times he came rushing over when I thought I had "lost" my book in the computer and he would retrieve it for me. Thanks to Blake, also, for his help with the many French phrases and references throughout the book. To Jimmy Roberts, I would like to express my appreciation for reprinting my entire manuscript on his computer when I could not. I want to thank my former fifth-grade students who would sit and listen to me attentively while I read the incident of the French children and popping the popcorn for them. Thanks go to Gwynneth Blackwelder for giving me this last and latest boost to "do something about that book!" To all my classmates and peers from the fantastic fifties with whom I shared so many marvelous times which provided the subject matter for the "flashbacks", I want to say "Thanks for the wonderful and warm memories." I am grateful to Cindi Daggerhart Lewis and David Blackwelder for their help in designing the cover for "Popcorn, Paris, and Paper Napkins." My mother is gone now, but had she not saved all the letters I wrote home during those sixteen months, this book would never have been. My heartfelt thanks and appreciation to my husband, Johnny, who never complained during the many months I spent writing in composition notebooks and then rewriting the entire book. For his encouragement and patience, I am forever grateful. I truly thank God that He has given me such wonderful grandchildren who will someday, by reading this book, glimpse into their grandparents' youth and behold an entirely different perspective of them.

INTRODUCTION

This is a love story, not only between two people but between those two people and a country. It is the heartwarming account of a young couple as they began not only a new life together but in a foreign country as well. World War II had ended thirteen years previously, and the people of France were more than ready for their "special forces," the Americans, to be on their way. The French were prepared by now, they felt, to protect themselves should any surrounding country become a threat to them. Arriving on this scene is a handsome young private in the United States Army with his even younger and naïve eighteen-year-old bride. Neither of them had been much farther than the small town of Cherryville, nestled in the shadows of the Appalachian Mountains in western North Carolina, which they called home. How their families, friends, and environment had sheltered them from the realities of the outside world emerges as they struggle to make a place for themselves not only in the army but with their French neighbors as well. Coping with situations that many would have shunned, these two faced with a spirit and determination that one can almost pity, but not help but admire. From being chased out of French places to accepting the integrated army and its citizenry, they were true ambassadors, without ever realizing it. They spread their love wherever they went in spite of the obstacles that stood before them. You will share their love, their hopes, and their dreams as you enter in the hallowed estate of matrimony with them. You will smile at the ofttimes humorous events remembered by the girl of life back home through flashbacks and the many events encountered by these two on the foreboding soil of France. You will be touched as heartbreak penetrates their very beings. But whether you are riding a motorbike, slipping into a French dance, or pretending to drink "vin rouge," you will be subtly impressed how these innocents, but determined friends to all, tenderly claimed a country, and the people of that country relentlessly claimed them.

FLYING HIGH

As the plane's propellers began to twirl faster and faster and the engines' roar became louder and louder, the plane slowly began its maneuvers to taxi down the runway. I overcame my temporary frozen state of fear long enough to peer out the porthole of a window and forced a smile to the horde of waving relatives and friends below. I was actually scared to death but was hoping that none of them had suspected the tug at my heartstrings. I had tried to put on a brave front as they all had gathered around me, wishing me well, hugging, and kissing me good-bye. It was not until then, surrounded by them, that I suddenly realized I was indeed going to France! Not only was I now leaving everything and everyone familiar and dear to me but would not see them again for over a year! The feeling the bride experiences to suddenly change her mind just before the wedding was nothing to what I felt now, trapped in this monstrosity of a machine carrying me to some unknown destiny. All the enthusiastic and assuring speeches I had given the army sergeant, family, and friends seemed somewhat obscure now as I was in actuality on my way. On my way, what beautiful words. I said them over and over to myself. On my way, but on my way to what?

Only three short months ago, I was coming down the aisle to receive the long-awaited high-school diploma, along with the other forty-seven members of the class of 1958, and, at the precise moment, secure in the knowledge that in exactly ten days I was to be married. The world had suddenly opened its doors; and I, so completely filled with optimism, eagerly, but blindly, was ready to step through.

Johnny, the boy to whom this flight would eventually take me, was the most wonderful person in the world. He was good-looking, sweet, considerate, and loving. He was everything a girl could ever ask or hope for. He had been a hardworking farm boy and performed his chores faithfully day after day before and after school. He loved his family dearly and had had no immediate plans of leaving them until the United States Army changed his life. He was sent to Fort Jackson, South Carolina, for his basic training and from there to Fayetteville, North Carolina, where he would remain seemingly for the remainder of his career in the army. It was during this time that we had started dating even though we had known each other in high school. As in most small towns, ours was typical in that everyone knew everyone else from the time he was born and his parents and grandparents as well.

The night he had proposed, I had written in my diary these immortal words, "I was so excited I wanted to vomit." Events had taken place so fast from that night on, Johnny said later, he did not know what had happened. We had planned a fall wedding, but the phone rang at my house one day, which changed all this. Much to my surprise, after talking to Johnny a few minutes, his father had taken the phone and gravely said, "Brenda, Johnny has something to tell you but just hasn't the heart to say it." In seconds, foreboding thoughts flashed through my mind, but mercifully, Garland did not hold me in suspense. "He is being sent overseas."

As this was peacetime and no war was going on to my knowledge, I felt such an overwhelming sense of relief that I immediately and emphatically replied, "That's wonderful. I'll go with him." This was before I had any idea of where he was going, when he was going, or if I would even be allowed to go. I simply knew I was going. Somehow, I could never quite understand the gravity of the situation. It never entered my mind that Johnny had thought I might change my mind about marrying him since he was leaving. But from the moment I had said, "I will go," all was well, and plans and arrangements were set up at a double pace. This meant I would be graduating, marrying, and preparing to meet my husband overseas practically simultaneously. And this is precisely what had occurred.

My mind reflected upon the hustle and bustle of it all. I had declined being a debutante, studied for exams, practiced for all commencement and class-night activities, attended bridal parties, and planned a wedding in less than six weeks. My mother was largely responsible for all of these being properly executed, for I was in such a constant state of bliss that I was of little use when it came to matters of hard-core reality. Being the romantic that I was, I had much rather daydream about such events, leaving the full responsibility to my mother. My dear father, confronted with all the extra confusing events, as I nearly always kept things in a state of confusion, came through with his usual fatherly wisdom.

"Brenda," he said, "you can marry this boy on the condition you can be with him, but I will not have you engaged on one continent and him on another." I have often wondered in retrospect if this were more than just fatherly wisdom or if in reality he had the sound judgment to know I would simply drive him completely out of his mind if I were tied down and left sitting at home. It was just not in my nature to sit at home, and he knew it. One can also quickly observe that neither I nor my father had a great deal of knowledge about Uncle Sam's army, for it would be decided in the final analysis by the army whether I would go and not us. However, the United States Army had never dealt with anyone quite like me before, and being a newlywed at that, the army never stood a chance.

"You are what we refer to as an unauthorized dependent," the sergeant yelled. "Can't you get that through your head?"

"I can be an unauthorized tourist, can't I?" was my reply.

"You will have to have many, many shots, my girl, and some of them can be very painful," he warned.

"I could stand a lot of pain," I stated firmly, "if it would help get me to Johnny." I secretly wondered just how painful it would really be.

He then tried a more practical approach by pointing out the financial aspect and reminded me that we would have to assume financial responsibility for my transportation.

"That is no problem, whatsoever. Johnny will pay my way," I stated matter-of-factly, knowing full well he had spent every last cent he had for my diamond.

Somewhat in vain, he said, "You'll never get through all the paperwork and red tape."

"Other people have, or they wouldn't be over there," I retorted.

In the end, the sergeant realized there was to be no way of discouraging me and admitted he was really glad I was going. It was his job to discourage unauthorized dependents, he explained. There were so many dependents in the area of France where Johnny was stationed that it was becoming more and more difficult to find suitable housing. He was a softie at heart, wished us luck, and conceded that once I got there, I was entitled to all privileges extended to other dependents, but it would not be easy for us.

I became fascinated with the fact I was actually on an airplane. I had been to the beach many times and to my mother's hometown in Tennessee, but that was the extent of my travels. Never had I dreamed of being on an airplane, and just as I was wondering how far away we were from Charlotte, the stewardess announced we were flying over Washington DC. I was utterly amazed! It would not be long until I would be in New York. It was good to know there would be friends there to help me make the change for the flight to France.

As I began to relax, enough to lean back on the headrest, I thought of only a few weeks ago when I had sent Johnny a wire, saying, "Coming, ready or not." His reply had been "Stop, letter to follow." How was I to know that due to the Lebanon crisis, he was spending night and day in the office, even sleeping on the desk at night? So my boast of going on even if I had to sleep on a park bench was closer to being true than I had ever dreamed. From then on, I had received such reassuring and endearing letters from him it had almost been worth the wait. Although his spelling was atrocious, his sincerity and earnestness could not be doubted for a moment. His greetings of "Dear Mrs. Stroupe [my wife]" "Hi, darling wife" or "My dearest love, Brenda" may not have been the most original greetings in the world, but to me, they were beautiful. After all, it was the first time I had been addressed as a "wife" by anyone, and I felt quite unique. That is how Johnny had made me feel from the beginning of our courtship: special, sweet, and unique. I loved him dearly for it. I smiled to myself as I thought about our honeymoon at his uncle's summer home at nearby Lake Hickory. We had had only ten precious days together before he had to leave. Oh, what marvelous and crammed-packed days of loving, learning, and discovering each other! We felt it is only appropriate to pin our marriage license over the head of our bed. It was as if we had to have it there to reassure us that all this heretofore forbidden behavior was, suddenly, after a thirty-minute ceremony, permissible and that it was quite all right for the two of us to be alone in this big two-story house.

I had cried when Johnny reminded me to boil the wieners in hot water instead of starting them in cold water. I was extremely sensitive about him discovering I could not cook, but he tenderly cajoled me into believing that my cooking was of no importance to him. We settled the entire incident by going straight up to bed with supper being readily forgotten.

Over the address system came the announcement that we were preparing to land at Idlewild Airport in New York. No one had to remind me to fasten my seat belt for mine had never been taken off. By now, my fright had completely disappeared, and sheer joy had taken its place. I now had several hours flying time on me, and I eagerly anticipated the next and bigger adventure which would be Air France, largest airline in the world, flying me across the Atlantic Ocean to Johnny. Everyone had tried to convince me that going by ship would be more pleasant and cheaper; but all I could think about was that we had already been separated for seven long weeks, and I wanted to get there the fastest way possible.

As I descended the steps from the plane, I spotted the familiar face of Johnny's closest high-school friend – Mike, who was in the air force and stationed at Fort Hamilton – in the crowd. He waved and motioned eagerly. Soon, I was hugging both him and his girlfriend and thanking them for being there. We talked of news from home, mutual friends, and my trip thus far. We talked about them and their plans for the future, and we passed the next hour or so in this manner. I was reluctant to bid them farewell as I, again, felt a lump in my throat and an uneasiness as I realized I was now getting ready to cross the ocean. I assured them of how grateful I was that they had come and met me. It had been quite a lift for my spirits to have a second send-off by someone from home here in New York City.

This flight was not only to be a long one but an endurance test as well. I did not have a seat near a window but faced a wall, which separated tourist class from first class. I was seated between two French-speaking people who conversed across me as though I did not exist. To make matters worse, all the announcements were given in French. When I realized the stewardess was giving instructions for an emergency in French (the only reason I knew this was that she was standing in the aisle wearing a life preserver), I felt totally ostracized. This was a new feeling for me but one to which I would soon become accustomed. I comforted myself with the thought that if we did crash, it probably would not make a great deal of difference whether I knew how to operate that life preserver or not. I went on to enjoy my first French meal and then slept.

ORLY FIELD

When I awoke, it was dark, and those around me were asleep. I felt a sudden pang of loneliness. I reprimanded myself by thinking about the vast difference there was between Johnny's trip and mine. In one of his letters from the ship, he had written how one fellow had gotten sick on the very top bunk; and before the ones below could get out of the way, it was too late, Johnny included. He had also said that no matter how seasick the men were, they had to meet their Kitchen Patrol duties. Some had been so sick they could not hold their heads up but had been carried off to the brig by the Military Police just the same. He had said they were so ill they did not care where they were anyway, but it seemed cruel and heartless to me. Fifteen days he had spent on that rolling and rocking old ship, at times having to stand and hold on beside his bunk, the seas became so rough. No one could convince me that going by ship would be more exciting; cheaper maybe, but from Johnny's descriptions, I could understand why.

I fondly recalled how Johnny had actually cried when he finally arrived, and all my letters were there, waiting on him in a bundle. He said he could just not help himself. He had not even chewed the stick of chewing gum I had placed in one letter but, instead, carried it on him in his shirt pocket. No one could possibly be as dear and sweet as my Johnny. I suddenly wanted to wake all the passengers on the plane and tell them all about him but decided against it as they would not be able to understand anyway.

Would anyone on this 125 passenger plane be interested in a young girl and her own personal love story? I made believe that they would. If

I could make those black-and-white attired nuns sitting there in the back understand me, I just knew they would get a smile or two from some of the antics I could relate to them about my honeymoon. Now that it was all over, I could even smile myself, even though it was disastrous at the time. The incident of which I was thinking about in particular had occurred during the middle of that week. Johnny had diligently instructed me on the various procedures involved in operating a boat, and I was quite pleased that I had succeeded enough to pull him behind me on skis. I had become so engrossed in keeping my eyes on the skier, which is an important safety factor, that I completely forgot to look where I was going, which is also an important safety factor; and before I knew what had happened, I ran the boat aground! Not only had I run upon land but Johnny had barely escaped being driven straight through the side of a nearby boathouse! He had dropped the line just in the nick of time as he saw what was happening. We had been very lucky that neither of us nor the boat was damaged. I was willing to bet those little ladies had never thought of anything like that occurring on a honeymoon. I surmised, though, that they had really never given much thought to honeymoons at all. Somehow, as much as I admired them, I felt rather sorry for them too. I could not imagine my God not wanting everyone to experience the kind of love and relationship I was sharing with another human being. The nuns seemed happy though, and I was confident that they could give me an entirely different viewpoint if given the opportunity; but I was glad at that moment that I was not Catholic, could not speak French, and that they were sound asleep and completely unaware of my thoughts.

How many hours now had it been since I left all those marvelous friends and relatives in Charlotte? They had all been wonderful in wanting to share this big moment in my life, and I loved them all that much more for it. Mother and I nearly panicked when we were informed that my luggage was overweight, and we had had a hectic time in the restroom, quickly trying to decide and sort out what I would need most. We had worked hurriedly and emerged with my clothes in a shambles but passing the weight test. I had absolutely refused to leave my books and wedding album and finally resorted to carrying two of the smaller books in my oversized pocketbook along with me. I could not imagine going to France without a book about the country, and the French-English dictionary was a must! Johnny had not yet seen our wedding album, and I insisted I'd leave my clothes behind before I would leave that album. Mother reluctantly agreed when she saw I meant it.

Johnny had written how difficult it was to communicate with the French people and what problems he had encountered trying to find us a place to live. I could picture him now, carrying the French-written note from door to door, explaining he was looking for a place for him and his wife to live. They had either shaken their heads no, or the place itself was so below any kind of lifestyle to which we were accustomed that Johnny had all but given up. The sergeant had certainly been right about the housing situation. Johnny had become so discouraged that he had said I must think him the worst husband in the world. I knew he was doing his very best though because I knew how much he wanted me there with him. His letters emitted a sense of urgency about them as more time elapsed, and we were still not together. He said he slept at night with my wedding picture right at his head and only lived for the day I would be there with him. It was only a matter of hours now until we both would be ready to live again. To be together – that was our most important goal in life. It did not matter where or in what we lived. Johnny said it made him feel better, knowing I had said I would live in a tent as long as I could be with him. I could not picture things being as bad as that and felt he only exaggerated so I would not be disappointed. He did not have to worry for a moment about me being disappointed, for I was determined not to be. Not for anything would I let him down about our new country, our new home, or our new life. Nothing could be disappointing about any single thing that had to do with us; of this, I was positive! He would feel better about the entire situation as soon as I was in his arms, and all would be right as soon as we were together. I wondered dreamily what his first words would be to me. I wondered what the French people would be like, how the country would look, and, most of all, what my first home would look like. I could not wait to get there!

"Please, God, please let all go well for us as we begin a new life together. We know that without loving you first, our love has no real meaning. Watch over us and take care of us," I silently prayed.

It was morning, and the man seated on my right had been kind enough to let me lean over him so that I could see the Atlantic Ocean far below. It was magnificent! Everything was magnificent – the plane, the clouds, the ocean – and the very fact I was a part of it all was almost more than I could possibly contain! I knew we were to arrive at Orly at eight o'clock Paris time. It was close to that time. My heart was beating so hard and fast I was sure I would explode any minute.

From the actions of people around me, I could see we were preparing to land. I could sense the excitement among the other passengers as they too anticipated whatever awaited them upon landing. And who would not be eager? Paris – Paris, France – the most famous city in the world!

Finally, we were circling the airport, and I realized we must be approaching the runway. Instructions were being given, which I could not understand, but I simply followed the actions of the others. Time was passing quickly now, and before I knew what had happened, the plane had slowly and haltingly come to a complete standstill. I did not know what took place during the next few minutes and was unaware of my actions. The next thing I knew I was coming down the steps, my eyes searching for Johnny. "What if he isn't here?" but I remembered his words from one letter in which he had said, "If I'm alive, I'll be there." And before I could think further, I spotted him far above and beyond me on an extended balcony for spectators. I could barely make him out, but there he was, waving wildly from behind the railing. He was carrying something, but I could not tell what it was. I first had to get through customs, and none of us coming from the plane were allowed to pass the first of a series of what seemed like endless gates separating us from the other side.

"Bievenue à Paris. J'espère que vous aimerez votre séjour ici."

"Oh, but I cannot speak French, and I do not know what you are saying, and I just want to get to my husband," I spilled out hurriedly and appealingly.

"Well," replied the now-laughing French customs officer, "I speak English and will get you through just as quickly as we can so that you can be with your husband! Does the young soldier over there, waving the bouquet of flowers over his head, happen to be him?"

Now quite relieved at hearing words I understood and feeling as if I finally had an ally, I proudly exclaimed, "Yes, oh, yes that's him" and whispered breathlessly, "Isn't he wonderful!"

We were in each other's arms in a few short minutes; and we hugged, kissed, cried, and laughed all at the same time. It was as though we were transfixed in time until we realized the flowers had been crushed between us. Johnny looked straight into my eyes, and the first words I had so dreamed about were "How much money did you bring?"

"Ten dollars," I replied, and we both laughed.

"Then, that's all we've got!" Johnny exclaimed.

We were in a foreign country, we were beginning a new life, and we were broke, but we had each other. Everything was perfect. I was on my way again; but to what? I did not know, and I did not care because I knew it would be all right as long as I had Johnny.

#####

Speaking The Language

From the back of the bus where I was seated, I shyly gave a little wave of my fingers to Johnny as he sat there beside a fat lady at the front. Because of the joy of being together and our extended greetings, we were the last ones to board the airport bus, which carried passengers to the train station. We had taken the last available seats on the bus: one near the back and one in the front. He would keep looking back at me as if to reassure himself that I was really there; and I would clutch the flowers, give a delightful little shrug of my shoulders, and smile in return. I felt like pinching myself to make sure I was not dreaming.

It was not long until we arrived at the station, and the first of several problems confronted us: finding and getting on the right train that would take us to Orleans, about sixty kilometers away. We stood for sometime, awed by the immensity of the station, the mass of people, and the general confusion surrounding us. I thought it an ideal time to put my few hurried French lessons into use given me by our local high-school French teacher. So anxious to prove my usefulness to Johnny, I proceeded to look around for a likely prospect. I spotted an elderly lady wearing a hat with a flower pinned to the band. I took this little flower to represent the closest thing to a smile I could decipher and gingerly approached.

"Parlez-vous anglais?" I smilingly inquired.

She quickly turned her head and mumbled something disgruntling.

Somewhat disappointed, but not to be thwarted at my first attempt, I turned again; but before I could speak, a young man asked if we happened to know where the restrooms were.

I squealed with delight and cried to Johnny, "I understand him, Johnny. Oh, I know what he's saying!" squeezing Johnny's arm and bouncing up and down.

"Brenda, calm down. I do too; he's speaking English!" He then tried to whisper, "He's speaking with an accent!" Then almost apologetically, he said to the man, "She's had a long trip and is very tired and excited." It was at that moment I realized I had never heard anyone speak with an accent. Johnny replied that we did not know where the restrooms were as I eased myself behind Johnny's back, nearly dying of embarrassment.

We finally purchased our tickets, and with the number of the train written on a piece of paper, we proceeded to go up and down the endless lines of waiting trains, searching for the correct train. As we were walking past one particular train, I looked up in astonishment to witness an act of which I had never seen the like in my entire eighteen years. For just ahead of me was a Frenchman, standing at the top of the steps leading into the train, urinating as nonchalantly as if he were in the middle of an Arabian desert with not a living creature within a thousand miles. I froze, as not only had the sight taken me completely by surprise, but the stream of urine actually blocked our way. The man did not pay us the least bit of attention but, instead, acted as if he were performing some divine work of art. I could not take my eyes off him as he just as nonchalantly refastened his pants, turned, and disappeared inside the train. I wondered for just a moment if he would wash his hands once inside. Johnny nudged me on and explained that the French were not known for their modesty, and I would get used to things of this sort. "Never," I thought to myself, "will I get used to anything like that!"

Johnny and I finally settled in a little compartment with seats facing each other. We were quite relieved at finally being able to sit down, and we eagerly made ourselves comfortable. Just as we got settled, we noticed a disturbance outside our compartment, and our short reprieve was rudely interrupted. There was much ado about us being in this particular compartment; we could tell that much. The conductor was having an animated discussion with several people and, at the same time, making urgent appeals it seemed for us to get out. Johnny kept showing them our tickets and pretended not to understand their gestures. Johnny stood firm, and finally, they all left. The two of us were more than happy to send them on their way and, at the same time, felt satisfied that we had at least won one round in the constant battle of communication.

My last thought before I dropped off to sleep with my head on Johnny's shoulder was that when I got back to the United States, I would be more than patient with any foreigners I might happen to meet.

#####

THE ARRIVAL

It was almost dusk when the train pulled into the station at Orleans. I was so tired that all I could think about now was just getting to my first home, whatever it might be. But as we stepped through the train-station doors, I felt as if I had been transformed into Alice from *Alice in Wonderland*. Fatigue vanished, for in front of me was a place that presented a fairyland appearance. Cobble-stoned streets seemed to represent spokes of a giant wagon wheel that spread in all directions with a lovely fountain and pond surrounded by beautiful flowers as the hub. The flowers and shrubs were arranged in an orderly pattern, carefully groomed to give a most pleasing design. Around all of these was a delicately made wrought-iron fence. The design of the fence itself was as lovely as the flowers and complemented their beauty. There was a small park to the right, and I could see a merry-go-round and other amusements for children. There were several wooden stands, which appeared to be concession stands. There were many buildings directly across the street with all of them having closed louvered shutters, covering what I guessed were the windows. All the names of the shops, buildings, and advertisements were in French, naturally, but only enhanced my wonderment. There was, however, a feeling of desolation about the place. There were no people in sight. It appeared that practically everyone had disappeared behind those closed shutters, and the only sign of life was a car passing now and then.

With the realization coming over me that this was my town now, my home, Johnny broke the magiclike spell by saying, "Welcome, Brenda. Welcome to Orleans, city of Joan of Arc. What do you think of it?" What did I think? I thought it to be the loveliest place I had ever seen!

He then picked up my suitcase, and I carried my raincoat across my arm and the flowers in my hand, and we made our way across the street to seek transportation to our new home. I was content now to let Johnny handle matters, and I busied myself by looking at the unfamiliar surroundings while I waited. He came back in a few minutes, carrying two bags of peanuts, and gave me the bad news that the buses had stopped running for the day, and our only recourse was to start walking. Our destination was an outlying village of Orleans called Saint-Jean de Bray, which was about five kilometers away. We started out immediately. I kept asking Johnny where all the people were, and he said the people just seem to disappear after dark. We stopped to rest by sitting on the suitcases beside the road and ate the peanuts for our snack. We had been so overwhelmed with the excitement of being together and trying to get to Orleans that we had completely forgotten about food. Now, here we were in France, a country renowned for its cuisine, sharing our first meal together: peanuts.

We were in this particular position when a friendly sergeant pulled to the side of the road and asked, "Need a lift?"

"Do we ever? Thanks a lot," Johnny answered, and before he had time to blink an eye, we had all our paraphernalia in his car, and the two of us were seated in the front seat along with him.

This was to be my first encounter with the unwritten law that seemed to bind army personnel with one another in time of need.

We soon arrived at Saint-Jean de Bray. The driver let us out, and we graciously thanked him, and he wished us luck. We said our good-byes, and the car pulled off and left us standing there alone once again. We must have made a peculiar sight as we made our way down the street, Johnny with a suitcase in each hand and me beside him with my book-laden pocketbook, raincoat across my arm, and the bedraggled flowers, trying to take in everything I could possibly see in the dimly lit streets. I could see that practically all the houses were behind high stone walls. Johnny said ours was similar. After walking in this manner awhile, he set the suitcases down in front of one of the entrances of the stone walls and unlocked the gates. "Well, here we are, home at last."

Home at last, it was unbelievable. I had left Charlotte, North Carolina, an eternity ago, or so it seemed. We entered, and he then unlocked a garage door, which I learned later was to be our entrance to the house. We walked directly past the little car, a Citroen parked almost directly in front of the door to our "kitchen," Johnny informed me. The "kitchen" was no more than a corner of the garage sectioned off by a thin partition. A lump formed in my throat as I looked at the moldy concrete walls, the bare table, a sink, and a contraption sitting on an upright orange crate, which I took to be the stove. It was no more than four legs about six inches high with two burners on top. There was no refrigerator!

It was all I could do to conceal my dismay. I must have managed to stammer out something pleasing, however, for Johnny was so happy at my reaction that he hugged and kissed me and said, "I knew you'd like it; it's so much better than some of the other places I saw."

Johnny eagerly put his arm around my waist and hurried me on up the steps to our other room. On the way, he opened a door right off the landing of the steps and pointed to a commode. There it was – setting in a small closet completely by itself. "We're lucky, you know, to have that!"

I agreed with him that it was convenient, but before I could ask him where the rest of the bathroom was, he pulled me on up the steps to a hallway.

We turned to the right, and there, at the very end, Johnny got out still another key and opened the door to a lovely bedroom. There was a high four-poster bed with a pink and white flowered spread and curtains to match. There was no closet but a tall wardrobe in which to hang our clothes.

"The French don't have a whole lot of clothes," Johnny explained.

"Evidently not," I thought as I surveyed the wardrobe.

There was a small closetlike room directly off the bedroom that contained a lavatory. This, I realized, was the rest of the "bathroom."

Johnny showed me every square inch of the room, eagerly awaiting my reaction. I was genuinely happy this time, and visions of our few household items, which were on the way, flashed through my mind. I had mailed them several weeks earlier and could not help but think what a touch of home our personal possessions would give the rooms.

We suddenly became keenly aware that we were alone and together once again. There was no ocean between us, no people, and no gates to separate us. We were here in our own little bedroom. It was late, and there would be plenty of time tomorrow to explore our new surroundings. We were both thinking of those nights in the big house by the lake. Suddenly, I dashed to the suitcase, scrambled around, and pulled out a surprise for Johnny – our marriage license. He quickly tacked it on the wall directly over our bed. It seemed to be kind of symbolic to us now, and Johnny was pleased I had remembered the license. This simple ritual seemed to reunite us, and we flopped across the bed and laughed heartily at our little special decorum. Our laughter soon died as we embraced and eagerly kissed each other.

Then Johnny showed me a gadget the French had devised. It was simply a switch hanging from the ceiling directly over the bed, which controlled the lights. One could flip the switch, which turned out the lights, and never leave the bed. I decided then and there that whatever the French lacked in modesty, they more than made up for in cleverness as the darkness completely enveloped us.

#####

FIRST DAY

I awoke the next morning to the sound of rain hitting against the closed shutters. I felt as though I were moving, gliding through the air with a motor purring somewhere in the distance. There was only a faint light in the room, and my mind was foggy as I tried to think where I was. I was lying on my stomach with my face buried in the pillow. I gently eased my head just over the right edge of the bed. As I did so, I eyed the rounded toes of a pair of men's shoes sticking out from under the bed, staring accusingly back into my face. To this totally unfamiliar sight, I awoke with a start and with the realization that someone else was in bed with me. I did not turn my head but, with my left hand, carefully reached out and "verified" this fact. Someone was definitely there. I swiftly then recalled the plane flight, the reunion, the bus, the train, and, finally, the night before. I lay there and thought, "We are together again; we really are, and we are ready to begin our life together here in France. It's true. I am really here with Johnny."

I wanted to make Johnny so happy that I was there with him, that he would feel it was worth every cent he had paid to get me there. I quietly slipped out of bed without disturbing him and tiptoed down the stairs to the kitchen. It seemed even worse than the night before as I took a second look by myself. There were only three old pots, two chipped cups, two bent spoons, and a few staples. I found a jar of instant coffee and pictured how pleased Johnny would be when I carried the coffee to him in bed. Now if I could only manage to operate the "stove." There was a bottle that contained something gaslike attached to the back of the two burners. I was so afraid I might blow something up that I decided against trying it. I went quickly back up the stairs and into the bedroom. The bed was empty. Johnny wasn't there. For a split second, a feeling of panic came over me. I quickly overcame this, though, as I realized he could not be far away, and at that moment, I felt a pair of hands quickly cover my eyes. "Guess who?" he playfully asked.

"Charles de Gaulle," I responded immediately.

"Wrong, guess again," he demanded.

"Well, as my acquaintances in France are far and few between, it must be Private first class John Stroupe" as I waited patiently to see if this answer would be acceptable or not.

"You're right, and for that, you receive a reward – a good-morning kiss!" as he turned me around.

After a quick kiss, still in a playful mood, he held me at arm's length and asked, "What do you mean by leaving your husband all alone in bed, little lady?"

"To bring his coffee, sir. I only meant to please him."

"And where is the coffee?"

I could hardly hold back my laughter, but hanging my head as if in shame, I apologetically replied, "I couldn't light the stove."

With this, we both burst into gales of laughter until it occurred to us that we might wake Madam Cassier, and we immediately quieted down.

We then went back down the steps through the garage and into the kitchen. Johnny patiently showed me how to light the burner. He then had me repeat the procedure by myself. I drew back each time I held the lit match to the burners as I turned the valve, which then caused it to ignite. Johnny got out a box of rice, and together, we managed to make two cups of coffee and a pot of rice. We each then drank coffee and took time about eating the rice from the pot with our spoons. As we had no means of refrigeration, there was no butter for the rice and no cream or milk for the coffee. However, we faced our situation with a spirit of adventure, thinking that if they (the French) could do it, so could we.

"We definitely need a few things right away, don't we?" Johnny stated matter-of-factly.

I was glad it was he who had been the first to mention it and not me.

"There's no denying that, Johnny, but just think how much fun we'll have buying some things and fixing up our own place," I said encouragingly.

"Honey, I was waiting for you to come so that you could get the things you wanted, but I was also hoping you'd have more money with you. We're practically broke, and somehow, we have to make it until payday."

"Johnny, doesn't it seem odd that you work in finance and here we are broke?" I tried to give our situation a lighter tone. However, he took me seriously and went on to say, "Working in finance doesn't give me any special privileges or any extra pay, little wife. Now let's get dressed and go to the caserne."

"The what?"

"The caserne is something like a miniature American city. It's the army post where there is a Post Exchange, cafeteria, movie, library, and army offices. It's like reaching civilization to us foreigners" as he winked and then got up from his chair. "Come on; you'll see," he said as he took me by the hand.

"How are we going to get there," I inquired, "as we have no car and no motorbike?"

"If we hurry, we can make the next bus; they run every two hours."

We hurriedly dressed, and I put on my white hooded raincoat. Mother was right in that she had insisted I carry it with me instead of sending it later. And so we set out, Johnny in his fresh crisp uniform with me happily beside him.

We walked a short way down to the corner of the street, and there waited on the bus. Luckily, the rain had slackened, and the bus was right on time. The people paid us no attention as we boarded and, in fact, became noticeably quiet as we took our seats. It became so embarrassingly quiet that I dared not even speak but nudged closer to Johnny. I smiled faintly, but their faces seemed frozen, showing no emotion at all.

"Why, they resent us being here on the bus," I thought to myself, "and they are deliberately avoiding looking at us."

The ride was not long, but even that had been too long for us. We had not spoken a word to each other. It was as though we were afraid for them to overhear us speaking English, and at the same time, we really could not understand why.

We got off directly in front of the caserne's gates. There was a cement wall about twelve feet high that stood from one end of the block to the other. At the entrance, Johnny showed the military police on duty his identification card and my passport. It seemed strange indeed to have to be "allowed" to enter a place.

After completing the formalities of getting inside, though, it was just as Johnny had said, an American town within a wall of cement. We walked up a street and passed several buildings, a United States Officers Club, and a theater. We then went into a cafeteria and sat down at a table. To our delight, a friend of Johnny's came right over.

"Well, if it isn't the newlyweds, Johnny and his bride. We all have been anxiously awaiting you, for your poor husband has been in such a state he has messed up more payroll checks than he has done right!" he said good-naturedly while slapping Johnny on the back and pulling up a chair from another table at the same time.

I noticed an accent of some type but did not utter a word as I at least knew he was speaking English and remembered embarrassingly my last encounter of this sort.

As it turned out, he was from New York City; his parents were Italian. Only Italian was spoken in the home, he later explained. He was both witty and friendly, and I immediately liked him. His name was Pete Gomaz. He had a moustache, which fascinated me. I had not seen many men with moustaches. I could not decide whether I liked it or not, and in the conversation that followed, I kept trying to visualize him without it. We talked amiably for sometime while eating scrumptious banana splits. I would sneak a look ever so often, while Pete was engrossed in conversation with Johnny, to see how the moustache was faring so close to the area consuming a banana split. Somehow, it managed to stay free of any telltale signs, but I decided in the final analysis that it would probably tickle like the dickens while kissing and was glad Johnny didn't have one.

During the course of our conversation, our lack of certain vital kitchen utensils (like spoons, knives, and forks) came up. Pete seemed interested, but the conversation moved easily on.

As we were saying our good-byes outside the cafeteria door, Pete handed me several items.

"Maybe this will help out the new bride," he said with a thick Italian accent.

"Pete, when and how did you get these?" I asked with surprise as I looked down at two forks, two spoons, and two knives and a set of salt and pepper shakers.

"Not for you to worry," he said as he went on his way, never once turning back to acknowledge my protest. I looked at Johnny, and he was just grinning.

"That's Pete for you, and you can't deny that we need them more than the army."

Johnny told me about each building as we passed. He showed me the commissary, where I would be coming to buy my groceries whenever we had the money, and a way to get here. I saw the finance office where he worked. As it was Sunday, we could not get inside. Johnny showed me a building used for college extension courses by the University of Maryland. I thought it wonderful that the men had the opportunity to further their education while serving in the army.

We then went into the USO Club, and he showed me the facilities there for the men's entertainment. There was an area for card games, chess, or checkers. There was also a darkroom and equipment for developing pictures. Johnny told me he planned to develop our pictures himself. He had always had an interest in photography and relished the idea of doing this. We could have gone to the movie except we stood a chance of missing the last bus to Saint-Jean de Bray. With the experience of last night fresh in our minds, we quickly decided against going to the movie and, instead, continued browsing about the caserne. I was truly amazed! Just as I had stepped from the plane into a different time and place, it seemed as if passing through these gates we had entered another. For here, in the midst of one of the largest cities of France, was a miniature American city. I was glad we had this place to rely on and a place where we felt we rightfully belonged, but the frozen faces on the bus haunted me. I vowed to myself that once we left this place and ventured again into the Frenchman's world, I was somehow going to break through the barrier that lay between us. "Dear God, help me make a friend, a French friend." I earnestly prayed.

And just beyond the high stone wall, I noticed a distant but shining rainbow arched against the sky.

#####

INTRUDERS

"Dear Folks," I seemed to be writing over and over during the next few weeks. I wanted to share every single experience, no matter how trivial, with them. I wanted them to see every new and strange thing as I was seeing it. I tried to write so that they would feel as if they were practically there. I possibly overdramatized some incidents so much so that by the time one read my letter, he was made to feel that just walking to meet Johnny was a momentous event. I would not admit to anyone, much less myself, that one reason for such a buildup of ordinary happenings was that, in reality, I was lonesome.

My favorite writing place was the wide stone window ledge. I would push to the outside the huge shutters that covered the windows, then unlatch the tall windows, which opened to the inside. I could then easily climb up into the window frame itself and sit quite comfortably with my back supported against either side. The ledge was of sufficient width for me to sit, and a railing prevented any danger of my accidentally falling. Directly beneath the window was Yuga's dog lot. Yuga was Madam Cassier's huge shaggy dog, which seemed to enjoy the extra company above him. Yuga and I spent many contented hours in this way, him sleeping below while I perched high above on the window sill and wrote many letters home.

Johnny had to leave early in the mornings and did not return until about six in the evenings, which left ample time to write letters. Also, Johnny had advised me to stay fairly close to the house for a while, at least, until we could make some friends. I had begun to think that this might be more of an improbability than either of us thought.

I proceeded to write vivid accounts of our everyday existence and attempted to insert sparks of enthusiasm into the challenge of "making do" with the little we had. I felt proud of Johnny when he succeeded in such endeavors, and I loved to tell the folks back home about them.

When it had become necessary that we find some means of bathing, other than the lavatory, Johnny devised a makeshift shower. The "shower" was simply a short hose and nozzle (such as used to attach to spigots to wash hair) looped over a pipe, which hung slightly below the ceiling in the garage. There was some degree of privacy in that we were allowed to use a small room directly off from the garage area for this purpose. It was damp, dark, and chilly down there, but it had to suffice.

I had gone down the first time, cautiously but bravely, to take my "bath." I peered into the cold-looking concrete blocked room, and I knew at once I dreaded it. I slowly and hesitantly removed my clothing and, in doing so, became more and more aware of the stillness around me. I could just not bear being down there alone, much less naked and alone, so I dressed and went quickly back up the steps to Johnny. I explained that I could not go through such an operation by myself and would he please accompany me.

"Would I? It will be my pleasure, ma'am" as he grinned from ear to ear. But then, he realized how truly embarrassed I was and quickly made atonements.

"I won't look, Brenda. I promise you I'll do whatever you want me to and not look," he said reassuringly.

"Not even a peek, Johnny. I mean it!"

"A gentleman's word of honor."

And so we agreed and proceeded together down the steps and into the "pit" as I secretly named it.

The ordeal was over quickly as I undressed and lathered up at a breakneck speed. Johnny, true to his word, kept his back to me while he turned on the water and waited for me to give him further instructions.

It was soon his turn, and we then switched positions, he bathing and me operating the spigots. He said I was not bound to the "gentleman's agreement" and could look if I so desired, but I gracefully declined. From that time on, however, it had been the "two" of us when "one" of us had to shower, which became more and more frequent. I told the folks about the shower itself and how clever Johnny was in making it, but I never mentioned that it took the two of us to operate.

I had become accustomed to the stove however it seemed odd to even consider it a stove; I could at least now light the contraption without the fear that I would blow something up. Our lot had improved considerably after payday in the amount of canned goods and staples we had on hand, but lack of refrigeration and an oven limited me as to what I could prepare. Our diet, therefore, consisted mainly of beans and rice. We were further handicapped in that Johnny could bring only a small amount home each day, and he refused to let me venture out alone. He was still thumbing to work each morning and returning in the same manner at night. It distressed me to have him do this, but he assured me it was a common practice. It was in this way that Johnny had become acquainted with a Sergeant Thomas. He told me that Sergeant Thomas picked him up frequently in the mornings and was warm and friendly. He was more than happy to help Johnny out when he could.

"Madam," as we referred to her, had remained somewhat of a mystery. She seemed to steal about the house during the day, and then each night at seven, she left and returned promptly at ten. Because of my inability to speak French, and her limited knowledge of English, our conversations quickly faded. One day, though, she had invited me into her kitchen for refreshments, which I readily accepted. As it had been so long since I had had anything cold, my thoughts were of an ice-cold drink and how refreshing it would be. However, I found myself trying to be sociable while sipping warm wine and not wince during the process. She seemed politely interested in viewing our wedding pictures, uttering oohs and ahs as she looked. She then showed me a photograph of a man who looked to be in his early thirties. I took him to be her husband. He had been taken from this very house by the German soldiers, and she had never seen him again. She managed to convey that to me. No words were necessary when I saw the tears in her eyes. I could see it was time for me to leave as she seemed to be drifting into another time and place. I gently squeezed her hand and returned somberly to my room. I then lay across the bed and cried myself. I remembered myself as a little girl, six years old, crying at war's end.

"Why are you crying, Brenda? This is a time to be happy." my mother had implored. "I'm crying for all those boys who didn't come back," I replied.

I thought of the terror that went through my mind as a child, seeing those German helmets during a newsreel at the movies.

And here I was, right on the ground they had walked upon, and right in a house into which they had come. I had touched a hand whose very being had been altered by them.

Johnny had come on up the stairs and into the room, surprised that I had not met him at the corner. After telling him about Madam's husband, he quietly said, "Brenda, has it ever occurred to you what a safe and secure life we have led?" We both sat in silence for a while.

"Let's go for a walk." he suggested. "You need to get out a little while."

This was sufficient reason to put on a fresh dress, brush my hair, and fix my face.

We stepped out into a pleasant September evening and noticed at once a buzz of activity going on across the street. Many bicycles and motor scooters were congregating in front of the building there. The French girls were riding on back of the motor scooters' sidesaddle with their skirts billowing and hair flowing in the wind. Their high heels seemed oddly out of place on the bikes and scooters. We couldn't help but be amused. They seemed happy, though, and we edged closer for a better look. We could hear the strains of music coming from the building within.

"Why it's a dance, Johnny. They're going to a dance!" I exclaimed. "Let's go, darling, oh please let's go!"

"We can't, Brenda. We'd be intruding; we have no business there."

"We do too! Look, it seems to be a community center of some sort, and we are a part of the community," I insisted.

"There's something I haven't told you about this community, Brenda."

"What . . . what haven't you told me that could possibly keep us from going to a dance?"

"There are rumors that this area is Communist, and that is why there are hardly any Americans living here."

"Oh, pooh, I don't believe that for a minute; and besides, everybody knows that Communists are Russians, and we aren't anywhere near Russia," I retorted.

"Brenda, you just don't understand."

"I understand enough that you don't want to take me anywhere. I'm stuck here night and day and can hardly step a foot out the door, and now here's a dance at our doorstep, and you're afraid of Communists! Well, I'm not afraid of them – French, Communist, or whatever. They're people, like you and me."

By this time, I was almost on the verge of tears, and Johnny relentlessly consented to go in. We agreed not to speak to each other once inside, just casually enter, smile, and utter a bonsoir when and if needed. Just maybe we could pass ourselves off as French.

We tried to act as nonchalant as possible while Johnny laid down the French money, hoping it was somewhere near the admission fee. Not a word was spoken as a few francs were returned, and we went on through the doors with the crowd. I was so excited I could hardly stand it. It seemed forever since we had been to a dance. It had been months. We began dancing right out onto the floor alongside the others. No one paid us the slightest attention, and we felt more at ease as time went on. To our delight, we heard the strains of "Only You" being sung in English across the room. We were under the spell of the music, lost in each other's arms, when suddenly the tempo changed, and a fast beat began. It was like sock-hop time in the United States of America, and we immediately started a swift mashed potato in jitterbug fashion. My arms were swinging, legs flying, and fingers snapping. We were so caught up in the music we were unaware that the others were beginning to form a circle around us. My eyes were half closed, and I was dancing away from Johnny and spun around just in time to catch the expression on his face. My heart skipped a beat as I sharply snapped back and as I realized the others had stopped dancing now and were watching us! My mind raced as I kept dancing while pumping Johnny's arm up and down for dear life. We swung into a side by side, and I whispered to Johnny, "Keep on; it's too late to stop." They were smiling and clapping.

We swung apart, and keeping in time to the music, we tried to dance our way toward a gap in the circle. We had all but made it when the music stopped. We were trapped! They gathered around, and the French words flew around us fast and furious. The crowd seemed to be in a jovial mood, so I hopefully replied, "Merci, Merci" when the jabber was addressed to us. It was too much to hope that we could get by, and we soon had to admit that we could not understand. Their expressions changed to angry looks. They began to talk loudly among themselves as if deciding the fate of the intruders. While they were thus engaged, we took this opportunity to ease toward the doorway. Once we got there, we struck out in a dead run for the safety of home. We realized they felt intruded upon, and even the optimistic me did not feel this the fitting time to enhance French American relationships. I couldn't help but smile later that night, though, when I wrote home, saying, "I bet they're still wondering who we were and where we came from."

BABY-SITTER

The chore I dreaded most was trying to wash sheets in the lavatory. Our things had not yet come from the States, and we were using army sheets, which were cot size, on our bed. To improvise – it was a way of life with us.

Johnny had positioned a rod across one end of the room so that we would have a place to hang our clothes. The wardrobe had immediately proven inadequate. For an ironing board, I used a suitcase with a folded army blanket and sheet on top. We wouldn't have had an iron except that I had brought a traveling iron in my suitcase. The traveling iron was unsuitable for Johnny's cotton army shirts, and when I accidentally ironed his pants with the creases going up the inside of his legs, he decided to take them to the post laundry. I was disappointed because I had really wanted to do his clothes myself, being an eager-to-please newlywed. He tried to convince me that it was to help me out, but I knew the real reason. The truth was, his uniforms were not presentable enough to wear after being washed in the lavatory and ironed on a suitcase.

We had carefully purchased a few basic items from the PX, and I felt better about my housekeeping. I now had a broom, a dishpan, and a few dishes. We no longer had to slice tomatoes with a razor blade or scramble eggs in a canteen cup. We now had a knife and a bowl at least.

Johnny had surprised me one day by bringing in two little plastic decorations for the kitchen. They were three-dimensional outlines of a fat French chef and a chic French waitress. We thought the plaques gave our kitchen just the French touch it needed. I put a gathered skirt around the edge of the sink to hide the bare pipes underneath. A tablecloth greatly helped the appearance of the entire kitchen, and I tried to keep several little flowers in a jar of water in the center of the table. The rooms had at least taken on a cheerful appearance in spite of the crude furnishings.

Johnny had come in one evening with concern written across his face. "Brenda, Sergeant Thomas' wife is sick and is being admitted to the hospital tomorrow. They have a problem though – the children."

"Oh, Johnny, I'd be more than happy to help out; in fact, it would give me something to do. I'd love it!"

"I told Sergeant Tomlin you'd feel just that way, so he's bringing the baby by here in the morning for you to keep."

"Oh, Johnny, you mean it? That's wonderful. I mean it's great! Just think how much fun I'll have with a baby. Is it a boy or a girl? How old is it?"

"I don't know much at all except it's a girl, and she's less than a year."

I had done some baby-sitting but not with any children that young. I tried to think what a baby would be like, what she would do, where I could keep her, and how I would feed her. I hardly slept that night for thinking about what the next day would bring.

The next morning, we were up early. I quickly washed the breakfast dishes and straightened up the kitchen as soon as Johnny left instead of going back to bed as I usually did. I hurriedly dressed and tried to read a little before the arrival. It seemed forever until I heard the buzzer, which signaled that someone was at the gate. I practically ran down the steps, out the garage, and through the yard to the entrance. I quickly unlocked the gates in eager anticipation, and there they were – a man with a baby in his arms. They were both looking straight at me through their big brown eyes, and I looked straight back – at their dark brown skin. Negroes! Johnny had not even mentioned it, not so much as a hint.

What could I do? Nothing, there was not a thing I could do but ask him in. I stared at the brown-skinned baby. "Oh my gosh," I thought. "what would they say at home?"

As he was giving me instructions about food, diapers, and her general schedule, I was only half listening. "Don't be ridiculous, Brenda," I thought to myself. "It's just a baby, an ordinary baby. The color makes no difference."

When he left shortly, seeming not to have noticed my surprise, I stared down at the little kinky-haired toddler waddling around before me. I had really not been exposed to many Negroes, except for some Negro women who, from time to time, had worked in our home. I knew they were different from us because they were segregated in all ways. They lived and went to school and church in a neighborhood of their own, they sat in the back of buses, they had separate water fountains, and they had to sit in the balcony of the theater. I had been cared for by them throughout my childhood, but never had I ever dreamed of a reverse situation.

As I was pondering these thoughts, the baby stumbled and fell on the garage floor, and I instinctively rushed to her as she cried out. I picked her up to see if she were hurt. She didn't seem to be but continued crying with tears trickling down her fat little round face. As I tried to console her as best I could, her little body pressed against my own. "Here she is, suddenly thrust upon a stranger, a white one at that. How confused and frightened she must be. Little one, I'll care for you; you need me as I need you, and I don't care what color you are," and I gently wiped her tears and took her right away to meet Madam.

THE REVELATION

It had been several days since the baby, Jeannette, had returned home. I missed her terribly for she had kept me busy practically every minute of the day. I had watched her constantly for fear that something may happen to her while toddling about. With her food being kept in jars and using powdered milk, the lack of refrigeration had not affected us. Madam Cassier had been more than willing to help us with an improvised bed. She had brought into our bedroom two large well-cushioned armchairs, placed them so that the front of the seats faced each other with the end of the arms touching. By further padding the bed with blankets and sheets, an almost-ideal baby bed had been made.

Johnny had enjoyed the time he had with his "instant" baby as much as I had. He said it was just great coming home to a little family. He would get down on the bedroom floor and play with Jeannette until she was completely worn-out. It had made me feel good inside to see them together. I had taken Jeannette with me to walk up the street to meet Johnny the several evenings she was there. On the last day, she had squealed with delight and almost jumped from my arms when she saw Johnny coming toward us. Then the three of us strolled back to the house, Jeannette in Johnny's arms.

I had written the folks that I was keeping a baby for a friend. I told them each cute thing she did, everything she ate, and the number of times I changed her diaper, but I never mentioned the color of her skin. I knew they would not or could not understand – I wasn't sure which. And the funny thing was that, to me, her color made no difference.

#####

Interrupted Honeymoon

The days seemed to go by faster now, and I could hardly believe a month had passed. Johnny would bring me little surprises home each day from work. If he didn't have a letter from home, he would bring candy, fruit, or something to use around the house such as a dishrag, potholder, or some similar items. When I would walk up to the corner to meet him, he would have such items hidden in his pocket or carry them in a paper bag. He was like a father, bringing home a surprise to his child each night. We both loved letters from relatives and friends, and Johnny would always wait until he got home so that we could read them together. The biggest surprise had occurred one day, however, as I was busily writing away in the window ledge. He had gotten home earlier than usual and was coming in the bedroom door almost before I knew it.

"Brenda, come downstairs. I do have a surprise for you!"

No further words were required as I jumped from the ledge, rushed directly by Johnny, and bounded down the steps in front of him. There were two large boxes sitting in the middle of the garage floor that I immediately recognized as the same two boxes I had so carefully packed and mailed from home almost seven weeks earlier. I knelt down beside the boxes and almost cried for joy.

"Oh, Johnny, our things. Our very own things have come!"

I could hardly wait until he pulled the boxes into our kitchen, and we quickly began cutting through strings and tape to get them open. It was a scene akin to the joy of Robinson Crusoe discovering boxes of goods washed ashore after being shipwrecked a month.

"Brenda, the electric skillet! You sent the electric skillet!" Johnny exclaimed as visions of fried chicken went through his head.

"Sheets, Johnny, pink sheets!" I exclaimed as I envisioned a pretty bed and held them up for him to see. "And matching pillowcases!"

"Your record player, you even sent your record player, Brenda. You thought of everything!" Johnny happily exclaimed.

"Here is the set of pots Daddy bought for my hope chest over a year ago, Johnny. Aren't they the most precious little pots you've ever seen?" My eyes began to water at the thought of my dad. Oh, how I missed him but tried not to let myself dwell upon it. As I looked lovingly at the pots, though, I couldn't help but reflect upon that particular bond that binds a father and daughter. I knew how happy and proud Daddy was of having Johnny as a son-in-law, but I also knew there was sadness beneath the surface that he had tried to conceal. Mother had confided to me that on our wedding day, after Johnny and I were safely on our way and the guests had cleared the house, Daddy sat down with his head in hands and wept like a baby. Johnny, of course, was never told of this. I understood, Mother understood, but Johnny might have felt in some way it was because of him, and this he must not.

Daddy had told some friends, half jokingly, that I would be back by Tuesday following the wedding on Sunday.

It had been on Wednesday, however, that Johnny and I were sitting on the porch of the lake house, which had been loaned to us, when we spotted a boat approaching our docking area. As we gazed out at the nearing boat, we made out three figures but could not identify them. The boat's motor had cut off and drifted beside the pier. Johnny walked down to see who the unexpected visitors might be. In a moment, he waved for me to come down. With anticipation, I eagerly headed toward the pier, straining my eyes to see who it might be. There, sitting in the middle of the boat, was Daddy! Before I could speak, he said, grinning from ear to ear, "I just happened to be passing by."

There he was on Lake Hickory, in a motor boat, a weekday at that, and just happened to be passing by. I never loved him as much as I did at that moment.

"Brenda, what in the world are you thinking about, sitting there with that ridiculous grin on your face?"

Johnny's words brought me swiftly back to time and place.

"I was just thinking about Daddy visiting us during our honeymoon, remember?"

"How could I ever forget? Came to check on his girl. You know, I think he's just the greatest. I can't wait till we get home, and I can really get to know him."

I knew Johnny couldn't have been any more sincere.

We went on and on in this manner for hours, looking and gloating over each and every item. We had a marvelous time that night, and it wasn't until we were in bed that I remembered to ask Johnny how he had gotten the boxes home.

"Sergeant Thomas brought me home and helped me get them inside, and do you know what else?"

"I have no idea, what?"

"His wife said she could have sworn that Jeannette tried to say 'Johnny' the other day."

"Why, Johnny Stroupe, you sound as proud as if she were your own," I teased.

"Maybe having one of my own wouldn't be such a bad idea," as he playfully pulled me beneath the covers.

#####

LITTLE DARLING

Johnny came home that evening with the exciting news that there was to be a company party on Saturday night.

"But how will we get there, Johnny?"

"Sergeant Higgins and his wife are coming to pick us up."

"That's wonderful! But gosh, I haven't been out in so long I won't know how to act."

"Come on, hon, we're going upstairs and brush up on our dancing!" as Johnny kissed me on the forehead, grabbed my hand, and led me up the steps.

It was not long before we had the record player going and dancing to "Little Darling" and the stroll. As we danced, we kept one eye on the clock, waiting for Madam's departure. It was difficult to "stroll" in the cram-packed bedroom, and as soon as she left, we felt as though the house were our own. When she was safely out and away, we opened our door, which led out into the hall. The volume was turned up as loud as it would go, and we "strolled" in time to the music right out the door. As we were dancing down the hall, Johnny's foot hit a potted plant, tipping it over. Relieved that the pot was not broken, we frantically replaced the scattered dirt as best as we could and swept out the remainder. Not that we had really done anything wrong, but we had just as soon as Madam remain unaware that we had strayed into her domain.

#####

OPTIMIST FOREVER

On Saturday night, the Higgins and another couple, Sue and Dee Ross, came by to pick us up. We were delighted when they accepted our invitation to come in before going to the dance. We were eager to share what little we had and even more pleased when they acted as if there were nothing at all unusual for six people to share two coffee cups. They patiently waited for one another to finish and washed the cup for the next one. They appeared more interested in us than in our circumstances, and I grew increasingly more at ease with them. Whether they were putting on an act to make us feel good did not really matter. We at least had people with whom we could commune, and they were doing their best to make us feel comfortable.

The Noncommissioned Officers Club was the most fabulous establishment I had ever seen. I whispered to Johnny that this must be how nightclubs in New York City looked. The floors were fully carpeted except for the dancing area in the center. There were leather-padded barstools scattered about the building. Round pedestal-styled tables circled the dance floor while tray-carrying waiters bustled back and forth, waiting on tables.

I was so enthralled with the surroundings I could hardly pay attention to the conversation being carried on at the table. When the others began ordering drinks, I told them that just having Coca-Cola in real ice would be the highlight of the evening for me. They all smiled sympathetically as Johnny explained to them how seldom I got anything cold to drink. Dee teasingly told me he would think of me and feel guilty every time he got an ice tray out at home. I laughingly replied that I was learning a valuable lesson in appreciation, and I was the one to be envied by them all. Dee whooped at this and said that I certainly needed no orientation to army life, that this was the same brainwashing philosophy of the army.

"My god, Johnny, they need your wife at boot camp! She'd prove invaluable. Can't you see her now standing beside a burly old sergeant as he sends the guys out on a ten-day bivouac with a pup tent and C-rations and her saying, 'Boys, you don't need a thing; you're learning a valuable lesson in appreciation'? And before it was over, she'd probably have the guys really convinced they were the lucky ones!" Dee said this as he slapped Johnny good-naturedly on the back.

I learned that Sergeant Higgins and his wife had four boys, each born in a different state due to the nomadic life of the army. Sergeant Higgins lacked only four years until retirement.

Sue and Dee were younger but also career people. This was Dee's second tour of duty in France, and he could speak French fluently. They had one child – a boy, Kenny – who was one year old.

I was fascinated with these people, their experiences, and the places they had lived. The army was something completely foreign to me, and they realized this. The closest contact I had had with the army was seeing the large posters of Uncle Sam pointing his finger at me, saying, "The Army Wants You" at the post office back home. Dee knew of someone getting ready to return to the States who needed to sell his car. With this information, we became quite excited. We needed transportation more than anything. The number of used American cars was limited, but they were traded among the service men as each completed his tour of duty. Dee said he felt we could get it at a good price, and he would even talk to the man for us.

We came home that night content and happy. It had been our first night out with others as a married couple. We talked until the wee hours of the morning. We vowed we would manage to save enough money for a car.

#####

BONJOUR

I had been studying from my French-English booklet given us by the army, and I would bonjour anyone and everyone I happened to meet. I was hoping just one of them might pursue further conversation, but somehow, it never occurred. What I would do if a person reciprocated never bothered me. I just knew I would manage somehow. It seemed that not one single soul in this entire village was the least bit interested in me, except for Madam Cassier, and after all, she was my landlady.

One afternoon, I had gone through the gate just a little beyond the enclosure to empty my trash. I saw, to my astonishment, four children gathered around the trash can, taking something from it. They scattered and scurried for cover as they saw me approaching. They had suddenly disappeared, but I knew they were all within hearing distance, so I jumped at the opportunity. "Bonjour," I called loudly. "Je suis votre ami." I waited. It seemed an hour passed but actually only a minute or two until the smallest one appeared. Gradually, each of them came from his hiding place and stood before me. I put on my friendliest smile and knelt down beside a little boy who looked to be about six years old.

"Quel est votre nom?" I asked slowly, hoping he would understand.

"Franswa," he hesitantly replied, and my heart leaped; I had made contact – he understood! He told me his name.

"Franswa," I repeated. He smiled. Then one by one, I asked each of them the same question.

"Martine," "Renee," and "Pierre," they answered in turn. Then the oldest one of the group, a girl, began talking excitedly as if trying to explain. Seeing the expression on my face, however, she realized I did not understand. I caught a glimpse of what she had clutched in her hand as she was talking and motioning. I recognized it to be, of all things, several wadded-up paper napkins I had thrown away previously. Once she stopped talking and our temporary verbal line of communication was broken, I made urgent attempts at motioning for them to stay where they were. While smiling to assure them of my friendliness, I flew inside to the kitchen. I grabbed a handful of fresh assorted-colored paper napkins and rushed back out, half expecting them to be gone. But there they were, still standing as I had left them. Their faces lit up when they saw the napkins. I could only guess that it must be the colors that attracted them. I divided the napkins evenly and distributed them to each child. How their little eyes shone, and one "merci beaucoup" followed another. I opened up the booklet to the phrase which read, "My name is" and pointed this out to them. Then, pointing to myself, I said, "Madam Stroupe." This seemed to amuse them, but they each, in turn, repeated my name. When they began to make gestures indicating they had to leave, I grew anxious at the thought of never seeing them again. I looked up the word for "tomorrow" and pointed to it. They then nodded their heads, "Oui, oui." I then found the phrase which read, "Quand reviendrez-vous," which again they understood. They then huddled together, and after a short discussion, Renee turned and held up two fingers, smiling. "Oui, oui," I replied, and we all smiled in mutual understanding. They would be back at two o'clock the next day.

I stood watching them as they ran away from me and on down the street with the napkins in their hands.

"They are beautiful," I thought, "just beautiful."

Johnny brought home chicken for me to fry that night. We had a delicious meal of fried chicken, rice, sliced tomatoes, beans, and coffee. The electric skillet had been a tremendous asset, and we were learning to manage without refrigeration fairly well.

Johnny heard about the children over and over that night, but if he tired of hearing it, he said nothing. He was only too pleased to find me excited and with something to which I could look forward.

The following day, I had everything prepared long before two o'clock. There was peanut butter on crackers and cookies on the table, awaiting their arrival. At exactly two o'clock, here they came. The girls had on printed dresses with apronlike smocks over them. Their socks came up to their knees, and their shoes, though somewhat bulky, were laced and tied with care. Their hair was neatly combed and their faces shining. I could see they felt this a special occasion, and I glowed inside. I said, "Entree" in the best French I could and proudly stated, "Servez vous."

They seemed to enjoy the refreshments even if they did only have water to drink. As they finished eating, I noticed that each of them carefully folded his napkin, as if for safe keeping, and placed it in a pocket.

They seemed to sense how sincerely interested I was in learning their language. It did not take long for them to make a game of pointing to objects about the room and having me pronounce the name of each object after them. They would giggle at my pronunciations. They would then tax my skill by skipping around and seeing if I could remember the correct name for an object they had pointed out previously. They laughed good-naturedly when I would make a gross mistake such as "water" for chair. I would then do the same to them with their answers having to be in English. It was only fair that they learn my language if I were to learn theirs; I managed to convey to them. We were laughing and playing our language game when Madam Cassier entered the garage in her little Citroen or the "Bouncing Betsy" as we called it. I stepped to the kitchen door and motioned for her to come in. She looked around the table at the children gathered there and pointed to me, saying, "You, mother." She then spoke briefly to the children in French and left. She returned shortly with apples for each of them. Shortly afterward, they began to say their good-byes. This time, there was no need for arrangements to be made. I knew they would return.

#####

THE ENCOUNTER

The children continued coming by practically every day, and we all were now a familiar sight, walking along the streets of Saint-Jean de Bray. The school, now in session, was just down the street from Madam's. I realized later that I had become acquainted with the children only a few days before school had resumed for the coming year. After that, the children came by at five o'clock in the afternoon when school dismissed. I felt sorry for the little ones having to go to school so many hours a day, but I learned later the children had from twelve o'clock noon until two in the afternoon for a lunch and rest period, which was some consolation.

I would often take walks while the children were at school and watch them through the gates as they played outside during recess. I somehow felt I belonged in school too, now that the leaves were falling from the trees. This was the first fall; I could recall not being happily engaged in the swirl of activities, which began each school year. Johnny had said it was only natural I felt like this. He said he had felt the same way during his first fall out of high school. I appreciated this, but somehow, it did not compensate for my situation. I felt a tinge of despondency and wished with all my heart Johnny did not have to be gone all day long. I envied him – getting to go to the office, working, seeing people, eating lunch at the cafeteria. I decided that there must be something I could do in this village even if no one would speak to me except several of the children. I happened to think about the little cafe on the main road. I had never been in there but had noticed it each time we got off the bus. A picture of an ice-cold drink came suddenly into my mind. What a treat that would be! I counted the few francs in my sweater pocket and felt confident this would be more than pay for a Coca-Cola. I had at least been here long enough to know that Coca-Cola was sold. My pace quickened, and I had soon covered the mile or so to the main road that passed through the village. There it was – "Café de Saint-Jean d' Bray." I hesitated for a moment. "Do I dare go in? Don't be silly; it's probably something like a drugstore at home," I thought to myself. Neither my thirst nor my pride would let me back down, and so I entered.

Once inside, I didn't know whether I was glad I had come in or sorry. The place was dreary, and the furnishings there were crude. Only a few tables and chairs were scattered about the room. Directly in front of me was a long bar with one man behind the counter, wiping some glasses. There were about a dozen men sitting about the room. Not one of them had even glanced up, but I knew they were aware of my presence. I felt as though I were the stranger entering the saloon in one of those cowboy movies. I gathered my courage and walked bravely up to the counter and, in the best French I could muster, asked for a Coca-Cola, remembering to say please.

"Oui, oui, mademoiselle," he said as he turned to get the drink. I hardly noticed he had referred to me as a mademoiselle instead of a madam for thinking how proud the children would be of me and my successful French request. He set an opened bottle of Coke on the counter. I paid, and he returned a few francs, and with this transaction successfully completed, I gained enough confidence to sit down. None of them had paid me the slightest attention, and I had begun to feel that my Americanism served as a protective shield. The Coke was so refreshing that I wanted it to last as long as possible. Just then, I was distracted by the voice of a man standing over me. He was old enough to be my father, and he sounded quite friendly. I said nothing but kept sipping my drink, hoping he would go away.

"Surely, he can tell I'm American," I thought. Then the realization came over me that maybe it made no difference to him whether I was American or not. He talked continuously while pulling a chair over to join me.

"Surely, he doesn't think I can understand him," I thought. By this time, I was almost in a panic. "Why had I come in here? What should I do?"

I shook my head back and forth, saying at the same time, "Je no compree."

He grinned and went right on as if he thought I was pretending not to understand him. I really could not understand him at all.

"I do not understand you," I blurted out in English and jumped up. I didn't know whether to be upset with him or not. I didn't know what he was saying. A look of surprise crossed his face, and his tone immediately changed. It seemed as though now he were trying to explain something, and I caught a hint of apology in his voice. I hurried out the door as the men's stares followed me. I was so humiliated I could die and began trembling all over. My face felt hot, and I could not control the tears brimming in my eyes. I just wanted to get as far away as quickly as I could. I was embarrassed, frustrated, and angry all at the same time. I couldn't seem to cry enough. It was childish, I knew, but I couldn't help myself.

There was a small park just ahead, and I hurried toward a bench there. I reprimanded myself going into the cafe in the first place. After further reflection, I came to the conclusion that it was all really my own fault, and I had no one to blame but myself.

"What is the matter?" a voice inquired. I was startled at the sight of a little girl standing before me and at hearing English being spoken.

"Oh, I didn't realize anyone was around," I said, slightly embarrassed. "Who are you," I asked, "and where did you come from?"

"You've got to tell me what's disturbing you before I'll answer," she insisted.

"Well, it's like this," I said while trying to pull myself together. "I'm homesick."

"Oh," she said, almost as if she were disappointed, "I've had that before."

"You have? Well then, you know just how I feel I guess."

"Oh yes, I know how you feel, but you'll soon get over it."

"I will?" I pursued, enraptured by this self-confident little girl.

"Of course, after you've been here awhile," she stated emphatically.

"How long have you been here?" I inquired.

"Just arrived, that's why I'm not in school, you see."

We both turned when we heard another voice calling from a house nearby.

"That's Simone, our maid, calling for me."

"Then you'd better go."

"I'll wait just a few minutes so she'll come out here, and then, she can meet you."

Just then, I spotted a French girl of about sixteen approaching us. She spoke English with an accent.

"Hello," she addressed me and then, to the little girl, said, "Alice, you must go now. Your mother wants you."

"Where do you live?" Alice asked me as she was preparing to leave.

"At Madam Cassier's, just down the street."

"We'll come and see you tomorrow so you won't be homesick anymore" and turned to Simone, saying, "Won't we, Simone?" It was more of a demand than a question. The French girl assured her they would, and Alice hurried on out of sight.

"Simone, what a lovely name," I said sincerely. "My name is Brenda Louise Stroupe, and I can't tell you how wonderful it is to find another English-speaking person living in this neighborhood. I'm trying to learn French, but it is difficult."

"I know," she said understandingly. "I thought I would never learn to speak English."

"You will bring Alice and come to see me, won't you?"

"Of course. I would like to talk more to you," she replied.

It was then I realized how little difference there must be in mine and Simone's ages. It would be wonderful to get to know her. I was also interested in Alice and the army life. Simone and I parted with the understanding that we would see each other soon.

With the meeting of Simone and Alice to distract me, I had temporarily forgotten the cafe incident. I thought it best not to mention it to Johnny but only tell him of the meeting with Simone and Alice. This way, the day would end happily, and I didn't want him to think he'd married a foolish girl, besides.

#####

CHINESE CHECKERS

Our little kitchen had become a hub of activity. Almost every afternoon, there were from four to eight children gathered there. They had even begun to bring their books and study around the kitchen table. It was with a deep sense of satisfaction that I busied myself as they studied and talked. As I looked at their happy faces, I basked in the knowledge that they were content in my presence despite our lack of verbal communication. They had brought me so many apples that I began making my own applesauce. The flowers they brought, no matter what kind or in what condition, graced the center of the kitchen table.

Alice and Simone had come to the house soon after we met in the park. Their company was especially welcomed because of my deepening interest in Simone. I was anxious to become acquainted with her, her country, and her way of life. I was eager to compare her thoughts and ideas with my own.

She and Alice would often come in the evenings when Johnny was at home, and the four of us would play Chinese checkers for hours. We learned that Alice attended the army school near the American post and was not at home when the French children came in the afternoons. I wanted so much for my French children to meet Alice and vice versa, but their visits never seemed to coincide.

We were delighted when Alice and Simone, with Alice's father and mother's permission, invited us to dinner at their house one night. Alice's parents were to be away for the evening, and Simone was happily planning and preparing a meal for us. This would be a treat for us, and we looked forward to it. We all made quite a special occasion of it. I took considerable time in deciding just which dress would be most appropriate. Alice and Simone were doing the same, and we all anticipated the event much as a child would on Christmas.

The time finally arrived, and Johnny and I happily set out walking up the street to the big house. We had barely rung the bell at the gate entrance when both Alice and Simone came bounding out to greet us. Simone kissed us each one on both sides of the cheek, and we reciprocated with the customary French greeting. Alice, acting the little lady she had been taught, was more reserved, but it was evident from her shining face she was as glad to have us there as Simone.

We were awestruck at the transformation once inside the two-story stone house. The outside appearance was much the same as the other French homes lining the street behind their high stone walls, but the interior was strictly American sprinkled with ornaments representing countries throughout the world. We were impressed too with Alice's knowledge of many foreign countries. She relished being the center of attention as she recounted event after event of either her own experiences or those of which she had heard. She proudly showed us her display of dolls representing each country her father visited.

After a delicious meal of chicken livers and mushrooms, baked potatoes, a carrot ring, and cucumber salad, we adjourned to the living room for coffee and dessert. We praised Simone ardently for her excellent cuisine, which she modestly acknowledged. We knew, however, she was pleased with herself and gratified by our compliments.

We played Chinese checkers for a while until Simone suggested we play some records. Soon, the four of us were dancing merrily about the room. Johnny and I demonstrated some of the latest rock n' roll steps from the States, and Simone and Alice undertook each step vigorously. We went on in this frivolous manner for some time, laughing as much as we danced. When it became evident that Alice was growing tired and sleepy, we immediately ended our activity as we ourselves were exhausted.

After Alice was in bed and asleep, the three of us talked quietly. Simone told us she was happy working for the colonel and his wife, but she became homesick at times too. It seemed to comfort her, knowing we too became homesick, but she reminded us that we at least had one another. She lived in a village about fifty miles from Saint-Jean de Bray and only got home about once a month. It was difficult, she said, to make arrangements for the trip home. She asked if we would like to meet her family sometime and go home with her. We wanted to, of course, but we were in the same predicament she was as far as transportation. We assured her we would like nothing more than to meet her dear family. By the time we were preparing to leave, the two of us felt a sense of kinship with this fifteen-year-old girl. It was with light hearts that Johnny and I strolled leisurely home that night.

"Johnny, you know we acted like kids tonight, don't you?"

"Depends on how you want to look at it, Brenda. There's nothing wrong with acting like a kid every now and then, is there?"

"No, I guess not, and I don't know when I've danced till I was dizzy."

"It was a good evening, hon, good for them and good for us," he quietly stated, "and I don't see a thing wrong with that."

"Neither do I," I quickly agreed. We went on walking in silence. "We've made two more friends," I thought, and somehow, the neighborhood seemed to have shrunk a little.

#####

YUGA

Fall was in the air. The evenings were growing cooler and the mornings becoming brisk. Johnny insisted there was no need for me to get out of a nice warm bed to go downstairs to the damp and cold kitchen. It did not take much encouragement for me to stay in bed. Johnny would dress quietly, kiss me lightly good-bye as I lay in bed, and close the door easily behind him. I pulled the covers about my head and comforted myself, thinking how much shorter the days would be for me. I would sleep until almost dinner. I then would fix myself something to eat, straighten up our bedroom and kitchen, and prepare to answer an ever-increasing number of people who had written us. Thus, I whiled away the hours, reading letters from home and writing letters to home.

About twice a week, Madam would invite me to accompany her to the city in her "Bouncing Betsy." This would have been an auspicious outing for me except for one thing: Yuga. Madam never took her car from the garage but that Yuga was not posed pompously on the backseat, which was barely large enough to accommodate an average-sized person, much less a monstrosity of a dog. He was so large that he would thrust his head through the sunroof located over the backseat. I had often been amused at the odd sight the pair of them made in the little car as they drove away. Yuga and I adored each other when I was perched above him, sitting in the window sill, and he was safely below in his dog lot. Yuga sensed my fondness for him, and when he came in contact with me, he could not contain himself. He responded in the only manner his dog's heart knew. This was by pouncing upon me, and while braced on his hind legs, he would then practically lock his front legs around me. In this position, he would proceed to lick me profusely about my face. I tried to fend him off, but he never took the hint. Once we were in the car, it was almost as intolerable. Instead of poking his head through the sunroof as he usually did, he would fondly prop his big wooly head on the front seat between Madam and me. He would feverishly lick my cheek and press his cold nose against my hair and face lovingly. As one might expect under such circumstances, rather than reprimand him, Madam seemed to take pride in the fact that Yuga liked me so well. It never occurred to her that I might feel any differently, and she coaxed him on that much more. I could not offend her by being rude to Yuga, so the excursion went – me shoving and glowering at Yuga when Madam was caught up in her driving, and smiling and petting him when her attention was directed toward us.

POPCORN

When the children had come by one afternoon after school, I decided to pop popcorn for them. As they nosily found their places around the table (it was necessary that they sit two to a chair), I began heating the oil to pop the corn. The children were chattering away while getting their tablets and books out to begin their work. Suddenly, they all got quiet. When I turned around, I saw that their eyes were wide, and each was staring at me as though they were astounded. Their expressions were ones of puzzlement, and I could not determine the reason for this unusual behavior. Then, like hailstones pounding upon a tin roof, the popcorn was bouncing and popping against the pot lid. Looking from the pot to the children, it suddenly occurred to me that it was this popping noise to which they were listening so intently. It was then I caught the significance of their queried looks. They had never heard popcorn popping. When they saw me began shaking the pot and pushing it back and forth on the burner, their bemused expressions turned to smiles and finally to laughter. They looked utterly amazed when I poured the white blobs from the pot into a big bowl in the center of the table. They looked from one to the other, giggling. I laughingly showed them how it was to eat, and there was hardly a moment's pause until they each had done the same. They were simply delighted! Before the afternoon was over, I had popped three more pots of corn. Upon preparing to leave, each one placed a small amount of popcorn in his or her napkin and wrapped the paper napkin securely around it as though it were some precious gem.

We had had so much fun; the time had slipped quickly by, and I saw through the window that it was almost dark. I decided to walk with the children down the street and see them safely home. As we were walking along, I noticed an attractive French girl on a motorbike approaching us. As she reached us, she swerved the bike to the curb and, while pointing her finger angrily at Martine, scolded her severely.

"Martine, ça fait plusieurs heures que nous te cherchons. Ta mère est très inquiète!"

I felt myself tense at once. It was I who was responsible for the children being late in getting home. I didn't understand the words, but I understood the tone. Frantically, I thumbed through the French-English handbook I always carried, looking for the word "sorry." I hurried over to the girl on the motorbike and stepped in front of Martine protectively. Pointing to myself repeatedly, I was trying desperately to indicate it was my fault and not Martine's.

The scowl transformed into a beautiful smile so quickly I was almost startled. A flow of familiar words, kind ones at that, followed.

"So you are the good American lady we have heard so much about. Martine has talked so much about the good American lady and her handsome man that Mama says her ears ache from listening," she said pleasantly as she held her hand out for mine. "I'm Nicole Roberts, and I'm happy to finally meet you. My friends call me Nikki."

"I'm Brenda Louise Stroupe, and I'm so glad that you speak English. It is all my fault that the children are so late, and I apologize."

"Mama has had dinner prepared for a while, and Martine is usually home by now. I am Martine's sister."

"Roberts doesn't sound French. I don't understand."

"I married an American three years ago. We now live in Missouri, and I am here on a visit home."

I could hardly take all this in. Here was a French girl who lived in America and was here on a visit to see her family. Before I could think further, she said she must take the children and hurry on home.

"Will you be home tomorrow about two o'clock?" she asked.

"Why yes, I'm always at home," I replied.

"I'll come for you and take you to meet Mama," she said as she pushed down on the motorbike's starter, making the motor roar. She then spoke to the children in French, and they scurried on as I waved good-bye.

I practically ran home. What news I would have to tell Johnny! How amused he would be, and surprised too, when he learned that the children did not know what popcorn was. The biggest news, however, would be about meeting Nikki. Johnny and I both reached the gate at the same time, and we both started talking at once. There seemed to be so much to tell each other, but this one time, Johnny insisted that he tell his news first.

"Save it till we get upstairs," I urged as he hurriedly unlocked the gate. Sharing the news of the day was something to which we both looked forward; and we eagerly made ourselves comfortable, sitting with legs crossed Indian fashion, facing each other, on the bed before we started.

Johnny's news was exciting. He told me he had a good lead on a car whose owner was soon going home. He had talked to the man, who was a friend of Dee's, and he had promised Johnny first chance at the car. He and his family were leaving for the States sometime in November. This would be ideal for us because by that time, we could have the necessary cash. We both were elated at the possibility of having a car.

Johnny was astonished that the children had never seen popcorn and wished he could have seen their faces. He was pleased too about Nikki and was as anxious as I was for the next day to come. Thus, we ended another day, just as we had many others, lying in each other's arms, anticipating the next day and the days to follow, wondering what each would bring.

#####

MAMA

True to her word, Nikki came for me soon after lunch the following day. We hit it off from the minute we started talking. We couldn't seem to tell the other one enough about oneself. For an hour or more, we talked in the little kitchen, and then I had proudly shown her our bedroom, which virtually was the total of our living quarters. She expressed approval of our efforts at making it cozy and cheerful, acknowledging, however, it was small. After looking around, she said, "Brenda, you'll need something to put on your head."

"What for?"

"To ride the motorbike. I am on the motorbike."

"You mean you're going to take me to your house on the motorbike?" I replied incredulously.

"Of course, and you'll love it. You'll wonder why anyone invented the car."

Love it I did! From the second the cool air came rushing into my face and the houses and shops became a blur as we whizzed past, I loved it! What a tremendous free feeling with the wind rushing past as we sped to our destiny. I held on to Nikki tightly and wished the ride didn't have to end. We stopped in front of a gate, which had a sign saying, "Electricis" on it. I was told that the sign indicated that Papa, Nikki's stepfather, was an electrician, his occupation.

"Mama," the name was meant for her. She was my ideal of a "Mama." She was quite a stout woman with a bib-type apron covering her large bosom and body. She looked up from her cooking as we entered the door, a broad smile spreading across her face. Her fleshy arms engulfed me in the next second. She was talking so fast that it was difficult for Nikki to interpret. Nikki finally gave up in exasperation and let her babble on, whether I knew what she was saying or not. It really did not matter, for the meaning was clear: she was glad I was there. We chatted amiably for the remainder of the afternoon, with Nikki serving as interpreter. She would tell Mama what I was saying and vice versa. Nikki said there was no French word she knew of for popcorn, but Martine loved it. It was then that Mama stood up in front of us and demonstrated what had happened to her with the kernels of corn I had sent with Martine to be popped. Mama had followed Martine's directions exactly, imitating the good American lady. Martine, however, neglected to instruct Mama on one important detail: to cover the pot! There she was, standing in the middle of the room, showing us what happened when the corn started popping. Her arms were going up and out over her head in rapid succession, showing us how the corn was popping up and out of the pot in every direction, falling in, on top of, and around anything in the general vicinity of the stove. I laughed until I was gasping for breath, and Mama was laughing so hard following her performance that tears were trickling down her cheeks.

As we began regaining our composure, I suddenly realized it was almost five o'clock, and I asked Nikki to take me home. Mama began speaking to Nikki hurriedly and gesturing with her hands.

"Would my husband and I come and eat with them before Nikki had to go back to the States?" Nikki interpreted the invitation for her.

"We would love it, oh yes, yes!"

Nikki related the reply, and Mama beamed.

It was drizzling rain as we rode home. The drops trickled on my face as we sped along. I began to think about riding on a motorbike in a real downpour or when the weather was really cold. "Maybe I do know why someone invented the car after all," I thought to myself, but I would never have mentioned this to my new and wonderful French friend. I just clutched her waist that much tighter as the rain fell upon the two of us.

#####

FRIENDS

The following days were busy and refreshing ones. Nikki and I spent as much time together as we possibly could. The reason she was here, of course, was to be with her family, which she may not see again for two or three years. I was aware of this and grateful for the time she and I had together. Nikki showed me around and told me where to shop, how to shop, what to do, and what not to do. She taught me how to quickly figure francs into dollars and how to pay for merchandise and to watch and count my change. She helped me with my French and encouraged me to speak it, no matter how absurd I thought I sounded.

Nikki would startle me just with the change of tone in her voice when haggling with the merchants at the flea market. She would spit out the French language as if it were fired from a machine gun. She always won, or so it appeared to me. She fought vigorously for a tea set I had taken an interest in, and before we left, it was mine. Nikki had seen to that. Not only had she bargained for it but had then presented the set to me as a going-away present.

If any of the Frenchmen made a pass at us as we walked by, she would either snap back at them with a sharp retort or, in some cases, make them laugh as we hurried on our way. As soon as we were out of earshot, she would tell me what they had said to us – some quite complimentary, she added. I found it somewhat uncomfortable, for I was not used to a place where every time you passed in front of men, you were subjected to suggestive remarks.

Nikki explained that it was an everyday French occurrence, and one learned to live with it.

"Brenda," she had said, "it would be an insult to us if they didn't flirt with us. They do it for fun and mean no harm."

I learned that she had met Jim, her husband, while working at the army base as a civilian worker. They had courted, married, and were now civilians living in Missouri. Papa, Martine's father and Mama's husband, was not Nikki's natural father. Her father had been killed during the war. Nikki remembered him only slightly. She did not dwell upon this but went on to say that this entire area had been completely taken over by the Germans during the war.

"This is why, Brenda, people here are suspicious of strangers and wary of soldiers especially. Many of the old ones see the Americans in uniform and feel the country is still occupied. They simply cannot comprehend that the soldiers are here for their protection."

CALENDAR COUNT

I sat up in the middle of the made-up bed, my legs tucked under me, studying the calendar carefully. I counted and recounted. Yes, something was definitely wrong or definitely right, depending on how one felt about the situation. I felt like shouting from the rooftop, "I'm late, I'm late!" as though no one else anywhere in the world had ever experienced anything like this. Well, I hadn't, and this was me. That was one thing I could count on: my period. It was like clockwork every month.

"Now, honey, don't get excited. There could be several logical explanations," Johnny admonished as he took a deep swallow.

"Like what, Johnny? I'm a girl, and I don't know of any other explanations."

"Well, for instance, just getting married, living in a new place, or something like that."

"But, Johnny, I know myself better than anyone else, even you, and I'm telling you that something is different, and I thought I should tell you," somewhat disappointed in his reaction.

"Listen, darling, don't get me wrong. I'm excited, all right? I don't mean that. What I'm saying is, let's not get all worked up over something, and it may not be so!"

"I have never been late a day in my life, and I wasn't late last month, and I tell you, Johnny Stroupe, we're going to have a baby!"

"That's great. I can't tell you how tickled I am, but, my gosh, Brenda, be sensible. One day late is too soon to tell! I don't know much about this kind of thing, but I don't see how you can hardly think about it. Months have different numbers of days, you have to consider that."

"All right, I'm sorry I even mentioned it. Just forget it. I won't bring it up again," I said poutingly. "Not for eight months will I say one word about it! Even when I blow up and look like a toad, I won't mention it. You'll have to see for yourself, and then you'll probably say, 'There's some logical explanation,'" and I burst out crying.

"Oh, Brenda, please don't cry. I can't stand it" as he tried to make amends. "I'll tell you what. I'll fix supper. You stay up here and rest, and I'll come for you when I'm ready" as he chucked me under the chin.

#####

DISCOVERIES

The next few days, I seemed to be floating on a cloud, for each passing day only confirmed what I felt in my heart. "Could it really be?" I kept asking myself. "Could there really be a tiny someone inside of me?" I had to be the luckiest person in the world! I not only had Johnny but I now had someone else, only this someone was closer to me than even Johnny was, for this one was with me every minute of the day and night.

Since Johnny and I had had our initial conversation, we had not brought the subject up again. I knew, however, that he was as conscious of the situation as I was, whether we vocalized it or not.

Such were the circumstances a week later as we prepared to spend the evening with "Mama and Papa." It had seemed only natural to call Mama's husband "Papa," and that was how it had been.

The house was buzzing with activity as we entered that night. There was a feeling of excitement in the air as Martine came running up to take our coats. Martine was delighted to have us in her house, it was evident, and she could hardly be still. After all, we were her "discovery." Mama was busy in the kitchen, making last-minute preparations with Nikki helping her. The two of them popped in and out every few minutes, checking on us. Papa spoke English fluently, so we did have someone with whom we could converse without having Nikki to interpret. Nikki's sister Pepee and her husband had also come. They had been married about a year and lived in a nearby village. They had come on motorbikes and planned to spend the night. Pepee was setting the table, which set in the middle of the dining room. The table looked lovely with candles in the center and a beautiful white tablecloth, which hung almost to the floor.

Finally, everything was ready to Mama's satisfaction, the wine was poured by Papa ceremoniously, and the eight of us sat down. One at a time, each course was served by Mama or Nikki. The meal began with a salad, this being replaced with a vegetable, and then another vegetable, and yet another, each being served on a separate plate. After completing one course, the plate would be taken up and replaced by another. I thought that there must be an endless number of plates stored in the kitchen, or Mama and Nikki would have to be washing at a furious pace to keep up with the demand.

We had been eating and drinking for perhaps an hour and a half when suddenly someone noticed that Martine was no longer at the table. We had all been so engrossed in our conversation; and with everything having to be interpreted, served to create some confusion, Martine had been overlooked. Mama went to Martine's room and returned shortly, motioning that she was not there. Papa called for her. No one was unduly alarmed at this time, but still, puzzled. Papa, all at once, began laughing out loud. While still laughing, he pointed beneath the table, motioning us to look. We lifted the tablecloth while still at our seats, and there was little Martine, lying sound asleep under the table. Papa picked her up gently. Martine, not stirring, was carried out by her father. It was not until Papa returned to the table and we all settled down again that the reason for Martine's sound sleep emerged. As Papa questioned each of the others, they began laughing uproariously. We looked from Nikki and then to Papa for an explanation. Papa then explained that with the excitement of having guests, and Mama being preoccupied, not one of them had remembered to weaken Martine's wine with water as they usually did. She had simply crawled under the table and gone to sleep, unbeknown to the rest of us.

When we finally finished the last course, it had been over three hours from the time we started. We had eaten leisurely, and the food had been delicious. Mama had demonstrated the meaning of "French cuisine." By this time, we felt perfectly at ease with this friendly and lovable group of people.

Mama and Johnny somehow got into a pantomime bullfight. Exactly how it started, no one seemed to know or care, but the next thing I knew, Mama and Johnny were in the center of the room. Mama had removed her apron and was holding it out to her side as a bullfighter would hold his cape. Johnny held his fingers beside his head as if they were horns and was pretending to charge at Mama. They were giving a marvelous performance. It was while they were engaged in this frivolity that I began to feel a little strange. I looked at Mama as she stood there, waving the apron back and forth as if she were antagonizing the bull. I began straining my eyes to focus on Mama and the waving apron when suddenly Mama became a blur before my eyes.

The next thing I knew, I was looking up at many faces as they stood around the bed, looking down at me. I looked from one to the other questioningly.

"What happened?" I asked. It was then I noticed Mama's expression. She was beaming and, with a gleam in her eyes, sat down beside me and proudly announced, "C'est un bebe, C'est un bebe!"

Maybe Johnny and I could pretend to each other that nothing was happening out of the ordinary, but Mama could not be fooled. My secret was no longer a secret. I looked up at Johnny as Papa heartily slapped him on the back, causing Johnny to smile broadly and shake Papa's hand. I knew at that moment everything was going to be all right. I sat up and put my arms around Mama, buried my face on her shoulder, and wept for joy!

SURPRISE

Several weeks later, I was quite startled in the middle of the day to hear the buzzer sounding repeatedly to the beat of "shave and a haircut, two bits" routine. I knew immediately that it had to be for me but couldn't imagine who in the world would be causing such a commotion or for what reason. I hurriedly put on my coat as I was rushing down the steps and through the garage, thinking all the while how upset Madam would become if she heard the gate buzzer being so abused.

"Thank heaven she's hard of hearing!" I thought as I ran toward the gate, crying, "I'm coming, I'm coming!"

I swung open the gate, and there stood Pete, taking his hand from the buzzer just in time to jerk his cap from his head, put the other arm behind his back, and make a deep bow.

"Pete, what in the world!" I exclaimed, and before I could utter another word, I spotted Johnny sitting at the wheel of a car across the street.

"A car, a car, is it ours?" I screamed as I went flying past Pete toward Johnny.

"Nobody's but," Johnny answered as I slid onto the seat beside him with Pete following. "Happy birthday, honey. A little early but happy birthday!"

"And I was going to escort the lady to the car," Pete said good-naturedly as he nudged me gently on the arm. "John, I don't see how you ever caught up with her long enough to get married."

"But, Pete, I was chasing him," I replied.

"In that case, I understand."

Johnny hardly took time to draw a breath for telling us about the car's features, all outstanding, according to him. I was so thrilled he would have had no trouble at all convincing me that the steering wheel was an outstanding feature.

"Hey, John, you're not trying to sell us the car," Pete said. "You own it. Let's take it for a spin. Watch out for crazy French drivers now."

By the time we arrived back at Madam's gate, I was convinced I was not just an owner but a proud owner of a 1949 Chevrolet coupe, which had been purchased that morning by my husband.

It was a marvelous feeling having our very own car, and I was left standing at the gate, marveling at the fact as Johnny and Pete drove off. We could go to the commissary and buy groceries, all that we wanted, at one time. We could go places now: movies at night, weekend trips, maybe even travel some. I placed my hand on my stomach and thought that if we were going to travel any distance, it should be soon.

We were going to have a baby, we had a car, and I would be nineteen years old the next day!

"Oh, dear God, thank you for life, thank you for love, and thank you for happiness. I've never felt so much of all three!"

Happy Birthday

I stood staring down at the beautiful chocolate cake with "Happy Birthday, Brenda" written in pink icing on top.

"Mother made it for you herself," Alice said, emphasizing the "herself." It was obvious that she was proud of her mother making the cake.

"It's beautiful, Alice; it's the most wonderful surprise I could ever have imagined," and I meant it. As I gazed at the flickering candles while Johnny, Simone, and Alice sang "Happy Birthday," I thought about the letter I received from my father.

He had seemed disturbed that I had not mentioned anything about being homesick in any of the letters I had written home.

"Did I not miss them? Did I not think about him and mother, my sister, and friends?" he had written.

If he only knew the times I was in tears thinking of home, he would never have doubted for a moment how much I missed them. I felt so guilty about my feelings of homesickness that I hid those feelings from the ones I was writing and from Johnny as well. I had tried to keep those homesick feelings deep within, for I didn't want to let Johnny down. I didn't want Johnny to feel that he was not making me happy in every way. The word "homesick" was just something we did not mention. Each of us seemed to harbor the idea that he might let the other down if it were ever admitted. Johnny, I reminded myself, had not lived at home for quite sometime before we left. He seldom brought up events that had happened at home in recent times. On the other hand, my entire life had evolved around my home until a few short months ago.

In order to keep my letters newsy and cheerful, I never wrote when I was longing for home. It had been a jolt to me to realize that I may have done the wrong thing. With this in mind, I had poured my heart out all the next morning on paper with a letter just to my dad. The more I assured him that I indeed missed them, familiar surroundings, and friends, the more despondent I became. I recalled my eighteenth birthday and how different it was from this one, one year later.

"You're going to be the homecoming queen, Brenda! We voted just a little while ago!" Nelson yelled as he picked me up and swung me around.

Some of the boys from the football team had come over to my house to tell me the news. They all came tumbling out of one car – excited, sweaty, and dirty-barging into the house.

The night I was crowned homecoming queen, the day before my eighteenth birthday, was one of the most special and sweetest nights of my life; I would remember it forever. But nothing would ever surpass the thrill I felt when the boys themselves came bounding out of that car, weeks before the homecoming game, to personally tell me the news.

That night, one year ago, I had never dreamed that in a year, I would marry, cross an ocean, and live in a foreign country.

Those memories only sharpened the nostalgia of this special day. How touched I was that a stranger, having never met me, had taken time to make a cake and decorate it for my birthday.

How I yearned to tell my father about the baby. I wanted to share this most important event in my life with him. I wanted to hug him tight and then say, "Daddy, I have the most wonderful surprise for you!" I knew, however, he would only become more anxious about me, and I did not want him to worry. It would be such a long wait too if I told them now. I knew the most precious and dearest sentiments would have to wait; it was the only sensible thing to do.

#####

THE MOVE

The children did not come by as often now as they once had. The weather was much cooler, and I knew they were in a hurry each afternoon to seek refuge in the warmth of their own homes. Mothers could be seen riding past on their motorbikes, going to pick up their children from school late in the afternoon.

Strangely enough now, the kitchen had taken on a drab appearance in spite of all I tried to do to brighten it up. The walls were dense with mold, even though we had recently painted. The windows, which were even with the ground outside, were impossible to keep clean. I was now actually becoming nauseous at the thought of having to go down to the kitchen. The one good thing that cold weather had brought, however, was an instant and natural refrigerator. I simply placed whatever items I wanted kept cold on the window ledge outside. Milk, butter, and other items stayed sufficiently cold and were in easy reach. We still had no ice, but we could at least have a cold drink. To me, this was a real treat.

Mama came by very excited one day, as usual, traveling on her motorbike. We had been a little disgruntled with Madam because she kept raising our rent and, at the same time, would refuse to turn up the heat. Neither would she allow us to use an electric heater as it would blow the fuses, or so she claimed. Simone had discussed the matter with her on our behalf, but it was of no avail. Each discussion simply ended with her crying, telling Simone how much she cared for us, as the rent continued to escalate. Mama evidently felt we were not being dealt with fairly either, for she had been house hunting for us. Johnny was at home early the day she came. She wanted us to follow her right then, that much was apparent, and follow her we did, she on her bike and us in our Chevrolet coupe. Somehow, we had not quite gotten used to seeing Mama astride a bicycle. As I had an American "Mama" image in mind, one baking cookies in a large cheery kitchen, it seemed rather odd to be following my ideal "Mama" as she sped along on a motorbike. But this was my French Mama, and she was leading us in earnest to somewhere she evidently felt was significant. We followed her through a large gate, and just beyond, we stopped. A robust, rosy-cheeked elderly Frenchman came out to greet us, and Mama looked upon us with pride as she introduced us to him. He and Mama chatted amiably back and forth in French. He would then speak to us in English.

It was obvious by this time Mama had brought us to look at a possible new place to live. I thought they would never stop talking and show us the place. The "place," it turned out, had been, in the past, a wash house of some type. It had recently been converted to two small rooms: a kitchen and bedroom. The rooms were quite livable, and we both liked them immediately.

"Johnny, we'd be by ourselves; we'd have our own two rooms out here where we'd at least not be under someone else's feet."

"It's really small, Brenda" as he surveyed the rooms.

"But a closet, Johnny. It has a built-in closet."

"Well, it is nice and clean, just being fixed up and all," Johnny said while pondering the matter.

"And look, Johnny, a shower in the kitchen. It has a shower!"

It did have a built-in shower stall, curtain, and all in one corner of the kitchen. The walls and ceiling were freshly painted and the floors shined. I wanted the place desperately, and Mama glowed because she knew we were pleased.

Johnny admonished, "You won't have a bathroom inside, Brenda. You realize that, don't you, hon?"

"Yes, yes, I know, Johnny," I said eagerly, "but I won't mind, honest I won't!"

There was one other matter that disturbed Johnny: a coal cooking stove. He asked the monsieur if a change could be made. He shook his head from side to side apologetically.

It was obvious now that Mama was asking what the problem was, and when he told her, a hot discussion ensued. The French fascinated me when they talked ordinarily, but to see two arguing with each other was something to behold. Our heads turned from Mama to monsieur while they gestured with their hands, their voices getting louder and louder. I could see monsieur's cheeks getting rosier still, but Mama would not be put down, this we could tell. Johnny and I were at a loss as to what was going on, but the argument ceased abruptly. The monsieur turned to us and said that if we decided to take the place, a gas stove would be arranged to compensate, he muttered, for any other facility the dwelling may lack. Mama had done it! We were satisfied and agreed to move immediately. The advantages outweighed the disadvantages, and in the final analysis, we knew we had made the right decision. In spite of Madam's pleas and promises of lowering the rent, we forged ahead. Besides, we were closer to Mama, and this gave me a good deal of comfort, knowing she was near.

We moved, taking everything we had in our Chevrolet. The children – Martine, Franswa, Renee, and Pierre – all came to help us, along with Mama. They all managed to find something to carry to the car for us. We were not moving far, but to us, it was a big event. Our two rooms were actually a low concrete building out by themselves. There was no stoop and no steps. The door opened directly to the outside. We felt secure, though, as we were still inside the high concrete wall, which surrounded the big house and the other smaller buildings around it. These smaller buildings had been converted into apartments, comfortable enough to house other military families. Several of the service people came over to greet us and offered their help. Coreen – a lovely, gray-haired older lady – and her husband, Roy, lived in an upstairs apartment at the end of the compound. He could retire in thirteen months, and they were counting the days. Vince and his wife, Bridgie, lived directly across the courtyard from us in a downstairs apartment. They had three children: Margaret, who was twelve; Mark, six; and Tim, the youngest, three. They all made us feel at home and glad that we were there. Most of these, we later learned, were waiting on government housing, which would be available as other American families were returned to the States. Because of Johnny's rank, we were not considered for government housing at all. We did not mind. We felt as though we had our very own little house. We were pleased to have a closet, instead of a wardrobe, and the kitchen cabinets were a joy. We had a real shower, even if it was in the kitchen; and I had an honest-to-goodness stove, an oven, and four burners. How glad we were that Mama had spoken on our behalf for that. I couldn't wait to bake a cake for Johnny! I had not given the outdoor-toilet facilities much thought. I had never used an outdoor "privy" as I knew they were called at home, but to me, it was just another challenge and was something to which I was becoming accustomed. "Surely, I could conquer a toilet," I thought to myself as I headed outside with a determined spirit.

CHRISTMAS SHOPPING

It would not be long until Christmas. We were reminded of this constantly when we went to the caserne. There were signs all about reminding us to shop and mail early if we wanted presents to arrive stateside in time for Christmas. Christmas decorations had hung gaily since October in the PX to enhance the Christmas spirit and to encourage Christmas shopping. There was nothing I enjoyed anymore than buying presents for someone else. I liked for a present to be quite special, and with us being here in France, I wanted the gifts we sent home to be unique. Our budget was tight, but we had managed to save some money for Christmas presents. We had agreed it was more important to send each one at home something than to buy for ourselves. Johnny gave me full responsibility for deciding on the right gift for each person at home, and I couldn't have been happier with the assignment. Johnny and I thought of making a tape for the family, telling them about the baby, but decided against it. Somehow, it seemed impersonal to make such an announcement on a tape and, perhaps, upsetting their Christmas and all. Secretly, I wanted my father to be the first to know and not everyone at one time anyway. We agreed that we would wait until after Christmas for our announcement.

I was delighted with the gifts I had purchased to send back home. Johnny was too, for his blue eyes sparkled as he looked at everything I had spread out on the bed for him to see.

"What did you say this thing is?" he asked.

"A camel saddle. I've heard Mother say she'd like to have one. She's going to be so surprised. I'd love to see her face when she opens it."

"Yeah, Brenda, that's just what everyone needs, a saddle for a camel," he joked.

This was to be for both her and Daddy as it had cost more than I had planned. It was perfect, however, so I didn't mind. There was a French music box for each of our sisters, a cuckoo clock for Johnny's parents, and a big Raggedy Ann doll for Johnny's niece. For others in the family, I had gotten handkerchiefs with something symbolic of France printed on them, such as the Eiffel Tower or the Arc de Triumph. There were small bottles of French perfume and souvenir spoons with "Orleans" printed on them. I knew they would all be thrilled with their gifts.

It was our first Christmas as a married couple, and we were determined each of them would have a gift from us, no matter how small. We wrapped each gift individually in Christmas paper. Then the hard job came of packing them all carefully in one large box and getting it prepared for mailing to the United States.

By the middle of November, all my Christmas shopping was over, and the presents I was so proud of were now out of my hands and on their way. I had had such a grand time of looking and deciding on the perfect gifts that now I felt a little sad. For me, the nicest part of Christmas was already over.

GRAVEYARD GIRL

We had received the most heartrending letter from my father I thought I had ever read. What he wanted most for Christmas, he implored, was a telephone call from us. He would love for us to call on December 20 during a party he and mother were having at the house. My heart ached as I read and reread the letter, knowing this was an impossibility. Tears trickled down my face as I hesitatingly began the task of trying to explain to him why.

"First," I wrote, "is the time factor. Your time, seven or eight at night, is three or four in the morning here. As we are constantly under a curfew, we are not allowed to be out after midnight."

I further explained, hoping against hope that he would understand, that we would have to make this call from Orleans, five miles away. Another problem was that the charges could not be reversed, and we simply did not have the money to pay for a transatlantic call. I repeatedly stated our love for them, only to find myself becoming more and more upset.

"Besides," I wrote, "we love you so much that I would cry on the phone and for days after."

I knew the real reason was that I wanted so much to tell them about the baby, but at the same time, I did not want anything to spoil their Christmas. Johnny and I both had remembered the fatherly wisdom of his pastor during the marriage-counseling sessions. The one thing he had stressed was that we should not have a baby anytime soon. He advised that it was good for two people to have some time to get to know each other before sharing their life with another.

"Kids, the one thing that you do not want to happen while you're overseas is to have a baby," he stated emphatically. "It would place an undue hardship on the two of you and, under the circumstances, could make for a hapless situation. Consider your families and how they would feel with you over there and the worry it would cause them," he had cautioned.

These words were ruminating in my mind as I painstakingly expressed my regrets for not being able to make a call and, at the same time, declared our love to them.

A melancholy mood came over both Johnny and me for the next few days. Knowing the mail was taking longer to be delivered because of the holidays, we just hoped and prayed that the letter would get there before the date of the party during which they expected our call.

Several events occurred shortly afterward, however, which served to lift our spirits. Our former high-school principal, Mr. Cranford, had written us a personal letter. Enclosed with his letter were six additional separate pages, each a letter written by present high-school students who served as office assistants. These were filled with the latest school news and gossip. Having served as Mr. Cranford's assistant myself, I realized that he had requested the girls write us while each was working her time in the office that day. Johnny, having only graduated two years before, knew many of the people about whom the girls wrote. We zealously read and reread the letters. Oh, how I missed the hubbub of high school! I had been into everything, including some extracurricular activities I perhaps should not have been. Just reading their letters brought back fond memories, and I let my mind wander deliciously to events that now seemed a lifetime ago but were, in reality, little more than a year.

"Keep quiet, stop making noise back there, or you girls are going to give us away," warned Gary, the driver of the Chevrolet station wagon.

"We can't help it; it's getting hot back here under these skirts," Sara replied.

"*Shh, shh,*" I tried to whisper but was so tickled I was about to burst.

There we were, four cheerleaders crunched together, hiding under our circular ankle-length cheerleading skirts, which we had taken off in order to create a cover of sorts, hiding in the rear-end section of the station wagon. We were anticipating, listening to the conversation that would soon take place between the four boys up front and a girl of notorious reputation in town. Because she lived directly across the street from the cemetery, she was called the "graveyard girl."

"She'll do it with anybody they say," said Kevin. "Everybody's going to her house, blowing the horn, and picking her up."

One aptitude that one can attribute to being developed by living in a small town is entertainment creativeness. When there is none, you create your own. Such was the case on this particularly boring Friday night after suffering an embarrassing football loss. For lack of nothing better to do, several of us girls had pleaded with the boys to let us go along to graveyard girl's just to see what would happen. The plan that evolved was that the boys, who were like brothers to us, would ride in the passenger seats, and we girls would hide in the extreme back section on the floor. That way, we could eavesdrop on the kind of conversation boys would have with a girl of this caliber.

The horn blew three times, which supposedly was the signal for sex wanted as soon as possible.

We were now doubled up with laughter and trying to stifle our giggles.

"Shut up – she's coming. She's coming out the door!" Michael warned.

"Ye, gads," Shirley whispered, "she's coming. She's really coming!"

Crouched low and under the mass of dark blue corduroy, we knew the graveyard girl could not hear, and besides, she was talking into the front-seat passenger's window.

About that time, a hand reached over the back of the seat and pushed our heads down farther, and from underneath one of the guy's breath, we heard, "We're gonna kill yawl if you don't shut up!"

This just made it more unbearable, and we proceeded to become more tickled until we could barely contain ourselves. At that precise moment, we heard her say, "I'll take all of you on for five bucks"; we could hold it no longer. We were managing to keep our heads and bodies crouched down, but we burst into peals of laughter. With that, Gary, the driver, spun away from the curb, getting a wheel at the same time, leaving nothing but black tire marks and a perplexed and disgruntled girl behind.

It had taken awhile for the boys to get over that incident, especially when we girls dedicated the song "Ain't That a Shame" to them in the *Cherry Leaves*, our school newspaper. This injured their pride, and they sulked for weeks about the whole episode.

"Brenda, what are you thinking right this minute?" This was a game Johnny would play with me at times, and he was usually intrigued by my answers. "You've got that look on your face again, like you're somewhere else."

Unsure of Johnny's reaction to that little episode, I quickly replied, "I was thinking about my letter to Mr. Cranford and how I made France sound like a dreamworld."

"Gosh, is that all? I'm a little disappointed. You usually have something on your mind farther out than that; what's so funny about that?"

"Well, do you think maybe I've misrepresented things here a little, like not mentioning that we don't have a bathroom, a television, a telephone, and other things they might think are necessary in a dreamworld?" I smiled. "They say they envy me. I thought that was kind of funny."

He playfully reached for me, grabbed me around the waist, pulled me close to him, and kissed me on the lips.

"You're terrific, Brenda; you have made it a dreamworld. It's a dreamworld for me anyway, having you with me. I love you more than anybody. I love you, I love you, I love you!"

"Me too, me too!" I cried as I squeezed him that much tighter and begin kissing him at the same time. With the letters dropping to the floor, we eased toward the bed, and I blushed as I wondered what Mr. Cranford and the girls would think if they could see us now.

####

CHRISTMAS SPIRIT

Another event that rekindled our spirits was an idea that Johnny and I both agreed was a marvelous one indeed. We decided to give a Christmas party for the American children that lived within our compound and the French children we had taken under our wings.

I could hardly wait for Johnny to get home that Friday afternoon. He had a list of supplies that would be necessary for our party that he was bringing home. Before he got home, however, I had an unexpected surprise.

Hearing a commotion directly outside the French doors to our bedroom, I pushed the curtain back just enough to see what was going on. There were Simone and Alice, dragging a small fir tree about three feet long, which I recognized immediately was to be our Christmas tree. The door was thrown open at once, and I ran out to hug them.

They were quite pleased with my reaction, and the three of us began immediately to make a place for it in the tiny kitchen. Conveniently, Colonel Boyce, Alice's father, had mailed two cross boards under it to serve as a stand. The three of us quickly began putting the one string of lights on the tree that had been given us by Bridgie, one of the American wives. She had said she could at least donate a string of lights and a few Christmas ornaments for our children's Christmas party.

"Popcorn, Brenda, popcorn," Alice said eagerly. "Do you have any?"

"Sure I do. You know I'm always going to have popcorn around for the French children," I responded. "As well as myself."

"Let's pop and string it then!" Alice cried while jumping up and down and clapping her hands simultaneously.

Simone was delighted with this idea; and before long, the three of us were working away, me popping popcorn and Simone and Alice using a needle and thread, stringing the fluffy white balls. Thus, the afternoon passed happily, and by the time Johnny came home, we were more than ready to show off our masterpiece.

The little Christmas tree made the little room – former wash house – simply glow. There was a feeling of complete joy that evening as Johnny and I hosted our first party. The fact that we were host and hostess to American children of the service families in the compound and our French children with whom we had befriended and vice versa could have mattered less. The children played games, laughed, and talked with Simone acting as interpreter when necessary. All of us were filled with what I perceived to be the true meaning of Christmas.

#####

THE BOX

Nothing was any more exciting than to receive a box filled with things from the States. This would stir excitement within us like nothing else. It was as if we were touching a part of home when we could take something from the box that a loved one had packed for us weeks before.

One afternoon, in the middle of December, Johnny came driving through the compound gates, blowing the car horn unmercifully. Everyone inside the enclosed area was aware that monsieur did not approve of a great deal of noise; so with this in mind, children came scurrying from everywhere, knowing something special was going on. The car had hardly come to a stop before Johnny was running around the corner to our living quarters with the children following just behind.

"It's here. Come on out quick. Our Christmas is here!" he cried out to no one in particular, and then to Mark, he said, "Go get your dad. I need him!" I ran to the car and looked in the backseat. There was a box so big I wondered how he had gotten it in the car at all. Shortly, Vince, Bridgie's husband, came over, and together, he and Johnny got the box into our little bedroom. With all the children looking on, we pulled out one gaily wrapped Christmas present after the other from its place in the pile of torn newspaper strips where it had been carefully placed. The children begged us to open the gifts right away, but we said in no way would we open a single gift before Christmas. They had such fun watching us pull every gift from the big box that several of the children turned the box upside down and emptied all the paper stuffings to make absolutely certain that not one other parcel remained hidden in its depths.

On Christmas morning, we took all our wrapped presents over to Sue and Dee's to spend Christmas with them. There, we unwrapped our gifts.

It seemed almost everyone from home had the same idea; to get us matching things. We received matching shirts and matching pants from my parents. Johnny's parents sent us sweaters alike. One of my aunts sent us flannel pajamas, and another one sent us bedroom shoes. There was stationery, envelopes, stamps, and pens from yet another. Johnny's older sister, Joanne, sent two homemade fruitcakes, homemade fudge, and assorted nuts. We were elated with our gifts and had a grand time admiring them, with Sue and Dee looking on. We were just as elated at seeing Sue and Dee's little boy, Kenny, having fun with his things from Santa Claus. This was how Christmas Day of 1958 was spent, sharing memories of Christmases past with those whom we were with while thinking poignantly of loved ones back home.

A Queen Of Sorts

The following weeks passed quickly and happily. We were invited
to more of the French children's homes for both meals and visits. Both
the parents and children could speak some English, and I was trying
desperately to speak French. When these efforts were exhausted, we
then resorted to hand motions and drawing on paper. Somehow, we
managed a fair degree of communication. We realized we were getting
special treatment by being asked into their homes, and we appreciated
being allowed to share intimate times with them.

An incident occurred one evening while we were guests of Pierre's
family that neither Johnny nor I ever knew the meaning of but enjoyed
just the same. The children had gone to bed, and the adults were having
cake and coffee when suddenly I bit down on something hard in the
cake I was eating. Since the object was too large for me to try to
conceal my surprise, the others were aware of it immediately. At first, I
was embarrassed, afraid the others might be upset, but when they
started applauding and laughing, Johnny and I too became amused.
Then to our amazement, someone put a crown of some sort on my
head. It was then that Johnny and I realized the object was definitely
meant for someone to find in his or her piece of cake. We never
understood the significance of the act, but it really did not matter; we
had played an important part in something that, evidently, was special
to them.

The service people with whom we were friends could not understand
why we enjoyed spending time with people whom we could barely
communicate. These were men and women well seasoned in the life of

the army. They were accustomed to foreign assignments. The way they dealt with living in foreign countries was to ignore the people for the most part and avoid their way of life as much as possible. Their way of coping, or so I observed, was to have everything around them as American as possible and especially not become involved with the foreigners.

I saw things an entirely different way. We were the foreigners. It was that simple in my eyes. We were living in their country; and I wanted to see, do, and become a part of it, at least for the time I was here. Nothing would ever change the fact that Johnny and I had already spent our first half year of marriage here and, as it appeared, would celebrate our first wedding anniversary here. More importantly, our baby would be born here, and he or she must certainly know something about the country in which he was born, and that was a fact.

MY PRAYER

The time had finally come, we felt, to share our miraculous news with the folks at home. There was a definite bulge in my tummy now, so much so that there were some dresses I could not wear and I had to be selective about what I wore, being sure there was enough room around the waist. Fortunately, sack dresses were fashionable at the time I left the States, and they were certainly coming in handy for an altogether different reason now. Our American and French friends were all happy for us, but informing our parents was an entirely different matter. Johnny agreed to let me handle this however I saw fit. We simply had to inform my family and his that they were going to be grandparents! At the same time, we must reassure them that everything was going to be all right. In spite of our joy, we had the unsettling feeling that we had let them down, remembering not only the preacher's advice but others as well. We wanted them to be as happy as we were but were not sure how this news was going to be accepted. My father had to be the first to know; of this, I was adamant! I would place this information in his hands and let him react and handle it as he saw fit. My father was a master, in my opinion, of making things right. I set about writing the most complicated piece of writing I had ever written. All the book reports, essays, and term papers put together were not as difficult as this was to be. I told my father, first of all, that he was to going to be a grandfather. I then told him that he would be the best there ever was. He would have to be because he was the best dad there ever was. I wanted him to be the first one to know so that he could tell whomever he wanted, whenever he wanted, and however he wanted.

With all the wisdom a nineteen-year-old could muster, I attempted to explain the impossible – the miracle of life itself.

"This was surely God's most precious gift, more than the creation of the earth and all that was in it, this miracle of life," I wrote. A tiny living being was inside of me that was a part of not only Johnny and me but his and Mother, Johnny's mother and father, and their parents before them.

I described how the doctor on my first visit had placed my fingers on a tiny lump in my stomach and informed me that that lump was my baby. Tears had begun to run down my cheeks right there as I lay on the examination table from the sheer awesomeness of it! That simple act of the doctor's had removed all fears I had had or apprehension I had felt about being in a doctor's office in such an unfamiliar position as I touched that tiny lump.

"Is it really, Captain Pearson?" I asked my doctor in a whisper.

"Yes, it really is," he said tenderly. "I believe you would have been disappointed if you had not been pregnant," he went on to say as he gently took my hand and placed it back by my side.

"Daddy, that's how I hope and pray that you and mother will feel," I wrote. "I can't begin to explain to you what an incredible feeling it is to be carrying this little life inside of me. Everything suddenly looks different; the world seems brighter and people seem happier. We just want all of you to experience this with us and for us.

"Johnny and I are not afraid at all. Why, just look at all the people in the world. They all got here the same way. It can't be that hard," I continued. "It's going to be a boy, Daddy. I just know that it is. He will be the son that you've always wanted, and I, Brenda, am going to give you that joy! I seemed to be pleading for understanding and approval at the same time. I so much wanted everything to be right." The line "While our hearts are aglow, oh tell me the words I'm longing to know" from "My Prayer" by the Platters kept running through my mind.

Johnny took the letter to work with him the following morning to be mailed. With a prayer said over it and all the love in the world inside of it, it was sent on its way. We then counted the days we knew it would take to get there and waited.

#####

THE LIDO

It had been awhile since Pete had been to the house, so when he appeared one evening, I was more than happy to see him. He always had a joke or something funny thing to tell that had happened in the office, so I naturally enjoyed having him around. He brought exciting news for us! He had a big surprise for the mommy – and dad to-be. He was treating us to a night out to the world-famous Lido nightclub in Paris!

"Movie stars go there, Pete!" I squealed. I was beside myself with excitement. Everyone had heard of the Lido. It was one of the must-go-to spots in Paris.

"It's going to be an all-night affair. First, we're going to eat at an Italian restaurant; then we're going dancing and then to the Lido. I'm paying for the whole thing, even the hotel," Pete stated proudly. Danielle, the girl Pete planned to take, was a secretary for Air France, the airline I had come from the States on. I could hardly wait to meet her and for Friday night.

"What in the world will I wear?" I wondered. Knowing Pete was a man of considerable reputation with both ladies and nightlife, I asked him for advice.

"Pete, will you help me pick out something to wear? I have no idea how to dress for something like that, and with this little stomach protrusion I'm having, it may be a real problem."

Pete and I together decided on a suit that I could still squeeze into. He assured me I would be fine in the suit as people wore street clothes into the Lido as well as dressy clothes. Whether this was true or not, I did not know. I was so excited, it did not really matter; we were going to the Lido!

Three couples made the trip that Friday to Paris. The third man, in addition to Pete and Johnny, was Italian also. He had a French date as well. The girls would, at times, speak excitedly to each other in French. The girls did not speak English, so Pete would interpret for us. Pete and his friend would sometimes do the same in Italian. I found it fairly fascinating that three languages were being spoken at one table; but we all managed to talk, eat, and dance and have a marvelous time, with language presenting no barrier. It was ten thirty before we went to the fabulous Lido. I was entranced with just being in the city of Paris at night. The lights, the sounds, the smells, the feeling of excitement that was in the air made my head swim. I gripped Johnny's arm tightly as we stepped in the Lido. It was the most incredible place I had ever seen! I felt good about how I looked also, for Johnny had bought me a brand-new dress for this special occasion. To be pregnant, I thought I looked pretty good. We were all so caught up in the goings on of the club that, at first, I didn't realize there was entertainment going on from the stage. Just looking at other people, what they were wearing, and what they were doing was entertainment enough for me. We were led to a table and seated. The waiter brought a bottle of "vin rouge," which Pete tested and, after his approval, was poured into our glasses. Not wanting to hurt Pete's feelings, I would pretend to sip the wine; then when the others were engrossed in the show, Johnny would switch his glass with mine. We carried on in this way quite inconspicuously until both glasses were drained. More wine was poured, and we proceeded to do the same thing once again. I squeezed Johnny's hand under the table as though we had really pulled off a tremendous caper. He squeezed my hand even tighter and, with a slightly red-faced little grin, winked at me.

"How I loved this adorable person next to me and how happy I was just at that moment," I thought to myself. About this time, as my attention was focused again to the stage, I saw something I had never seen in my life.

"My god, those girls are showing their breasts!" I sat flabbergasted for a few minutes; then I sneaked glances at the people around me, checking their reactions. They seemed not at all phased, so I tried my best to conceal my consternation.

"What a country," I thought. "Men use the bathroom anywhere and whenever they feel like it, and women strut around on a stage with high plumes on their heads while showing their busts! Furthermore, no one seems to think anything about it!" Well, our folks back home would probably walk out; but since we were Pete's guests, I said not a word, relaxed a little, and tried to concentrate on the choreography. My eyes, however, kept reverting to the women's breasts. I never dreamed they came in so many different sizes!

We left the Lido at one thirty in the morning and then rode all over Paris. We drove around the Arc de Triumph and up and down the Champs-Elysees. We saw the Eiffel Tower, the Moulin Rouge, and the Louvre. We didn't get in our hotel room until five o'clock in the morning. It was worth every minute of sleep we lost. We fell into bed completely exhausted but happy as any two people could possibly be.

#####

REJOICE

Johnny could hardly contain his excitement. He had in his hand what we both knew was the reaction from our families about our big news. How Johnny had managed not to open that letter all day was beyond my understanding. We had a practice of reading our letters from home together. It was kind of a little ritual. In this incidence, though, I thought it must have taken a great deal of willpower for Johnny to restrain himself from opening that letter at work. With trembling hands, I opened the letter and began to read it aloud.

They couldn't believe we had been concerned for a minute about all of them not thinking this the most wonderful thing in the world. As it happened, when the special letter arrived to my father, he was in bed, sick with pleurisy. Mother had read the letter to him, and they both had been so touched that they cried. We should have known them better, she said, than to think they would be upset and only regretted that we had spent any time at all, worrying about their reaction. She then described how they had gotten the letter on a Saturday morning. After the realization that they were to be grandparents, they called my little sister, Laurean, in to tell her. She had been secretly praying for this, she told Mother and Daddy as she ran out the door to tell her friends in the neighborhood. Mother got on the telephone and called everyone she could think of after she called Johnny's parents first. She called them immediately to share the news. They were all ecstatically happy, she stressed. No, they would not worry, she continued, as we had many good friends who were willing to help us.

A close friend of theirs, Berge, had come by to see my father that same day. Daddy had Berge reread the letter out loud. I could just picture them – Berge, sitting by Daddy's bed – reading that letter to him. Daddy was delighted, Mother said, when Berge described it as a beautiful letter and that Johnny and I would be wonderful parents. Berge was not only a family friend of ours for years but had taught both Johnny and me in high school. We both thought the world of him, so this extra tidbit of information was especially welcomed.

We were elated with this news! Our families now knew. We could now write to them about the most important thing in our lives.

As fate would have it, on the very evening we read that letter, something very special happened. We had finished eating, and I was attempting to embroider a bib for the baby. Suddenly, I felt a flutterlike movement about where my waist once was. I paused for a moment, and I felt it again. I practically yelled at Johnny in excitement, not being able to wait to tell him what I suspected. I knew I had never felt anything like this before. Being ignorant of matters involving pregnancy, I had just recently read about the unborn baby moving inside the mother. I thought this to be an astounding piece of information! Now, here I was, experiencing that phenomenal event for my very own self.

Johnny had all his field equipment on the floor, getting ready for an inspection the next day. As it happened, Vince came over to help Johnny with his layout. While he and Johnny were working, I felt it again. With this, I ran over to Bridge's. She and I sat and waited for just a while, and then it happened again. This time, the titillation was stronger and lasted longer. Bridgie and I could now even feel it with our hands! She and I ran back to my house so that Johnny and Vince could also feel this evidence of life. Off and on, all during that night, Johnny and I would wake up and place our hands on my stomach for signals from the baby that he was really there and a very real part of our lives.

#####

Soot And Gloom

Johnny came in several days later with a darling bassinet for the baby. He had gotten it for four dollars – mattress, lining, and all. We were so proud of it that we rolled it into the kitchen so that we could look at it while we ate. Immediately, after we finished eating, Johnny had to dash back to work. He was working extremely long hours due to end-of-month payroll, sometimes not returning home until one in the morning.

After Johnny went back to the office, I ran over to Bridgies, not intending to stay long. She and I drank coffee while I described the baby bassinet Johnny had brought home. I was so happy to have it but happier still that Johnny had gotten it himself. That made it all the more special, of course, and she agreed. I told her good night and started back home.

As I approached the glass french doors that opened into our bedroom, I noticed that the lights were out, and I felt sure I had left them on. I stepped in to turn the lights on when I realized the entire place was filled with smoke. I ran back toward Bridgie's, screaming for help. Bridgie came running out the door, yelling for me to get in her house and she would go for help. Monsieur Roche and Vince came immediately and ran toward our house. They came back and told me it was not a fire, but the entire place and everything in it was smoked up and covered with soot. They had set the Aladdin kerosene heater that we used to heat with outside. They surmised that a draft from the door caused the flame to go out, and it continued smoking. Vince was going to the post to get Johnny and practically ordered me not to go near our little home.

When Johnny finally got home, he and I, along with the neighbors, surveyed the damage. Soot an inch thick covered our bedroom and kitchen. Nothing had been spared.

"Johnny, everything is ruined – everything!" I cried. The tears started flowing down my cheeks as Johnny tried to console me.

"It'll be all right, honey, it'll be all right. Thank God, it wasn't a fire," he said with a quiver in his voice.

Monsieur Roche lamented that the ceiling and walls would have to be repainted.

Johnny assured him that he would do the painting.

"I'll do everything, monsieur, don't you worry one bit. I'll fix it, and you'll never know anything happened."

"Oh, Johnny, look at our precious little bassinet. It's horrible!" I cried.

"Brenda, that's the first item we'll get cleaned up and ready for you, you'll see," said Bridgie emphatically. "I promise you it'll be as good as new."

"You guys may as well plan to stay with us awhile," Vince stated emphatically. "There's nothing else to do. Now just come on home with us now; there's nothing we can do in here tonight."

Vince was right about that. The bed and the linens on it were covered in thick soot. All our clothes in the closet were even covered. Things stored in suitcases under the bed even had thin layers of soot on them when we opened them. Everything in the kitchen cabinets, items on the table, our utensils in the drawers – everything was caked with soot. We had to leave right then with not so much as an item of clothing fit enough that we could take with us.

For the next few days, our little house was a flurry of activity. All the military families in the compound, Monsieur Roche, even Mama and Papa, all pitched in to get our place livable again. They took the blankets, curtains, towels, clothes – anything washable – to one's homes who had washing machines. Bridgie washed the sweaters by hand; other items were sent to the dry cleaners. Johnny, Papa, and monsieur washed the walls, the ceilings, and the floors. The ceiling and walls had to be repainted. Johnny was given several days off from work when word was received of our dilemma. As I was not allowed to do any of the strenuous work, I was given the job of tending to the children while their mothers worked on our house.

In less than a week, we were back in our own two little rooms. Everything was spotless, including the little bassinet. Bridgie had certainly been true to her word about that. We were certainly grateful to everyone for all their help!

Shortly after we moved back in, our car began having trouble starting. Neighbors would come out each morning to push our car until the motor would turn over and begin running. If we had not just experienced such a traumatic event, it might have been comical, but under the circumstances, it seemed somewhat pitiable. Johnny would be all dressed in his uniform, looking quite spiffy in the driver's seat, while Vince, monsieur, and anyone else who happened to be up at that time of the morning would be pushing the car from behind. They would push and run at the same time until the car gained speed, would suddenly start, and Johnny would take off, waving good-bye. His fellow workers at the office would repeat the same scene in the afternoon.

Johnny and I would huddle together in the bed at night and discuss the recent trying times.

"Do you think God is punishing us for something, Johnny, that we have done wrong?"

"You know better than that, Brenda. God doesn't punish. God loves people. People can't always help what happens to them, but God can't be blamed either; sometimes it's just a matter of luck."

"I'm trying to figure out why, then, we're having such bad luck."

"People have been trying to answer the question 'why' since the beginning of time, Brenda; it's not for us to understand, but just believe," Johnny kind of whispered.

"Where's my little optimistic wife, anyway? I don't like to hear you say bad luck. Our home is all fixed up, and we'll soon get the car straightened out."

"I'm homesick, Johnny. I don't want to hurt your feelings, but I'm so homesick I can't stand it, and I want to see my mother, my daddy, and Laurean." There was no holding back the tears. I pressed my face into the pillow and cried. After my sobs had subsided somewhat, Johnny tried to console me, "Brenda, God, I love you so much and that little life you're carrying in there of ours. We're the luckiest two people in the world, remember that. Nothing bad is going to happen to us."

"I know, I know. I just can't help it."

"Hey, have you ever thought that maybe God is helping us to grow up and become stronger people through these experiences?" Johnny questioned.

"I guess that might be. Yes, maybe that could really be," I pondered. "Maybe so that we'll be better parents or something."

"Thank God that we have people at home that love and care for us and that we we'll see again. Thank God we've got people here who have helped us and care for us," Johnny said softly.

"And thank God that the baby and I are both healthy. See, he's kicking right now – feel" as I took Johnny's hand and brought it over to me.

"Gosh, he really is moving all over the place. It's like he's thumping here and thumping there."

We were both wide awake by this time; the baby was creating such a stir. The smoke, the car, and the homesickness were forgotten as we became caught up in wondering what this active little creature could be doing inside of me.

"Thumper, that's what we'll call it, Thumper. That'll be our little nickname for it," Johnny declared.

"Oh, Johnny, that was the name of the rabbit in *Bambi*. We can't call it that."

"This is because he's thumping in you! It doesn't have a thing to do with a rabbit. I say it's Thumper."

And Thumper it was. I came to the conclusion that a person wise enough to explain the logic of God had the right to call his baby any name he wanted to.

#####

PAPA

Mama came bursting in one day not long after the smoke incident with a handful of tulips. I'm sure she felt this would cheer me up, which it did. They looked quite pretty on the table in our freshly painted kitchen.

She had some recent pictures of Nikki, which she showed me. There was Nikki in front of a nice ranch-style brick home, looking as happy as she could be. I could not help wonder as I gazed fondly at her picture if I would ever see her again. I missed her tremendously.

I could not explain to Johnny later how Mama conveyed this to me, but before she left that afternoon, I knew that the American soldier living up the street from us had left his wife for a French girl. It was amazing how there seemed to be no language barriers when it came to the worldwide pastime of unadulterated gossip.

Johnny had come home with a message from Papa that evening also.

"Papa said to tell you he'll be here tomorrow afternoon. He has something for us."

I wondered what in the world Papa could possibly have for us. I at least would not have to wait long.

Papa did come the next afternoon as promised. He had three wooden boxes! I could not imagine what he intended to do with those boxes. He was quite pleased with himself, I could tell that much, and he instructed me to simply watch. He then proceeded to nail those boxes on the wall above the headboard of our bed. What a grand idea! This gave us additional storage and looked attractive as well. All we needed to do was paint them.

"Papa, we can't thank you enough. I don't know what we would do without you," I said, and I gave him a hug. He just smiled, gathered his tools together, and left.

I wondered to myself how we possibly could ever thank these people for what they did for us. Would there ever be a way we could convey to them how much they meant to us? "There was just no way," I thought. "No way."

#####

Spoiled Tourist

Everyone had been telling us for months that we simply must see the palace of Versailles. They said we must not leave France before we had seen it. As we now had our car operating again, due to a new battery and a new starter, we decided to go several weeks after the smoke ordeal. Things had slowed down for Johnny at the office, the weather was unseasonably warm, and it seemed the perfect time for just such an excursion.

I had tried to gather as much information about this historic palace as I could. "It was more interesting if you knew something about the history of a place before you actually saw it," I had informed Johnny. Without this knowledge, you could not fully appreciate what you were seeing. Johnny was not quite as enthusiastic about this way of thinking as I was but listened patiently to me as we made our way early that Sunday morning out of Orleans, northward toward Paris.

"Johnny, did you know that the palace itself is one-half mile long?"

"No, I didn't," he answered as he maneuvered the car in and out of traffic.

We could never get used to the idea that cars entering from the right into a main road had the right-of-way. It kept American drivers constantly on guard.

"Why, it has hundreds of rooms! Can you imagine that!"

"Well, no, I can't since I spent part of my life in a three-room house," he replied.

"Did you know that it was largely due to the life of luxury and the wastefulness of the court life at Versailles that the French Revolution occurred?"

"Brenda, to tell you the truth, I've never really thought about it. It was all I could do to manage a passing grade in United States history."

"But this is exciting, don't you think, Johnny? Can you just imagine how it might have been back then, the growing discontent of the French people and them begging for bread? Then that Marie Antoinette having the audacity to tell them if they didn't have bread to eat, they should eat cake."

"Marie who?"

And so we continued, me chatting amiably to Johnny, trying to feed him over two hundred years of information in a two-hour ride, and him trying desperately to contend with the notorious French drivers along the way.

No amount of historical information, written descriptions, or personal accounts by ones who had seen it could possibly have prepared Johnny and me for the splendor of Versailles! My mouth was agape as we stood at the elaborate palace gates at the entrance to the enormous courtyard, which stretched in front of the palace just beyond. I had never, in my wildest imagination, ever dreamed of such a place existing. For some reason, the tune "It's Only Make Believe" kept playing in my mind as we crossed the courtyard to enter the mansion. Surely, this was what Conway Twitty had in mind when he titled that song. We made our way, along with other tourists from all parts of the world, trying to grasp the splendor of this place. As we entered the Hall of Mirrors, we read that this was the site of the official ending of World War I. The fighting had ended when Germany accepted the armistice of November 11, 1918, but it was not until the Treaty of Versailles went into effect on January 10, 1920, that the war was officially ended.

"Well, they certainly could not have chosen a more magnificent place to end a war," I thought as we looked at all the brilliance around us. Elaborate artwork covered the ceiling and ornate columns lined both sides the length of the tremendous hall. Gold highlighted both the ceiling and sides of the hall, outlining the mirrors.

We strolled, awestruck, through the palace on out to the formal gardens, which formed intricate patterns on the enormous acreage. In the center of these gardens was a broad walk leading to a mile-long Grand Canal. I especially wanted to see the Petit Trianon, a favorite retreat of Marie Antoinette. I knew, from having read about her life, that the "little" palace had been given to her by her husband, Louis XVI, as a gift. It was there that she could forget about her responsibilities as a queen and be frivolous and do as she pleased. I couldn't help but think about this young girl, only fifteen when she had been brought from Austria, in a grand manner, to marry the son of the King of France! Then, to think how her life ended gave me the shudders!

I was getting tired after more than several hours of looking and walking, so I sat down on one of the benches in the garden to rest, telling Johnny to go on and that I would catch up. An American woman sat down beside me, and we began a conversation.

"Are you not tired, carrying around that extra weight and all?" she asked.

This being the most precious bit of extra weight I had ever had, I slightly resented the phrase "extra weight" but answered politely.

"Oh, just a little, but I wouldn't take anything in the world for being here and seeing this, would you?"

"Frankly, I'm sick and tired of seeing these old castles and gardens. After you've seen one, you've seen them all."

Her remark had stunned me so that I could not answer, and she continued, "Where are you from? Has to be from the South somewhere."

"I sure am. From North Carolina, in fact, but right now, my husband and I are living here in France. He's in the army!"

"You're actually living in this place? How can you stand it?" she asked incredulously.

"What could I possibly say to enlighten this dissenting woman?" I thought to myself.

"To be honest, we're very happy here. We came as newlyweds, and now, our baby will be born here," I stated rather proudly.

"Well, God help you. I'd hate to think I'd have to have a baby here. These people here are so unfriendly. I'd always heard the French were snotty, and now, I know it."

"Oh, but they're not," I wanted to say, but the words just wouldn't come out. I felt that this woman, no matter what I told her about our French friends, would only scoff at the suggestion that they could be friendly. I felt a little sorry for her. Perhaps she was spoiled, much like Marie Antoinette, and had been indulged in as a child. "Never, I hope and pray," I thought to myself, "will I go to so many places and see so many things that I would not be affected by the likes of what I was seeing today." I also wondered what kind of impression she had made upon the French people with whom she may have come in contact. If her attitude was an indication of how American tourists presented themselves, I could hardly blame the French for avoiding them.

I hastily bid her farewell, telling her I needed to catch up with my husband. I wished her a safe trip home. "Home, wherever that was, is exactly where she needs to be," I thought as I got up and hurried to find Johnny.

Over The Mountain, Across The Sea

Johnny and I were becoming quite clever with our improvisations. Since Papa had introduced the idea of using wooden boxes on the walls, we found all sorts of useful ways in which we could arrange boxes for extra storage. I was pleased with myself when I covered an orange crate with contact paper and set it directly beside the stove. I made a curtain, which hung on the front of it to cover the pots and mixing bowls that were stored inside. I used the top of it for work space. This worked out so well that I set about building a dresser of sorts from six wooden boxes. I sandpapered, painted, and then made a cloth cover for the front of these. Not only were these practical but could easily be disposed of once we left France to return to the States.

In order to cope with the ever-present mildew that seemed to appear almost everywhere from the constant dampness, Johnny lined the back and sides of our closet with a combination of cardboard and aluminum foil.

In addition, Johnny attached a wire from the radio outlet and connected it to a speaker box in the kitchen so that the sound of the radio could be heard easily in both rooms.

For the first time in my entire life, food seemed to be the first and foremost priority. Until this time, eating had been secondary, hardly being given a thought except for something necessary to stay alive. I had been so engaged in the demanding activities of a teenager that meals were simply something to be inhaled as quickly as possible so that I could move on to more pressing matters, like listening to the same record over and over. I fondly recalled how I would nearly drive my father out of his mind at times.

"Brenda, honey, if you want to keep playing that record player, would you at least please change songs?" my father yelled from the bedroom across the hall. "It's getting on my nerves, hearing the same one over and over."

"Daddy, I love it. Please let me play it just a little while longer. I'll turn the volume down."

"Over the Mountain, Across the Sea" had some mystique about it that completely captivated me. The words, the melody, the mood it set mesmerized me. I continued to play it several times more.

"For gosh sakes," Daddy's voice now boomed, "that damn song sounds like a funeral procession; cut it off!"

I knew when it was time to cut things off. He had had it; he had been pushed to the limit. I, therefore, reluctantly came out of my dreamworld and resumed working on my English homework without accompaniment of music, needless to say.

HEARTBEAT

I was now baking, thanks to my oven, goodies such as cookies, nutty fingers, banana breads, and even apple pies. Johnny was delighted with country suppers of cooked cabbage, hot corn bread, corned beef, and pinto beans. I never had the heart to tell him, though, that it was only after several of these country suppers that I found out that pinto beans needed to be washed before they were cooked. I was sitting in Bridgie's kitchen one afternoon as she was preparing their evening meal when I observed her rinsing the beans.

"Bridgie, why are you washing those beans?" I asked.

"Because, dear, they have dirt and grime on them; sometimes, little rocks are even in them. You need to rinse them well before you cook them, remember that," she advised with her motherly wisdom.

"Sure," I replied "I won't forget that" at the same time wondering just how much dirt and how many rocks Johnny and I had already consumed.

It never occurred to me that my being pregnant had anything to do with this newfound interest in food until Bridgie and some of the other more experienced mothers brought this to my attention. "Food will never taste as good as it does when you're pregnant," they said. I couldn't agree more.

I came out of the doctor's office, bursting with news for Johnny.

"The doctor heard the baby's heartbeat, Johnny. He actually heard it!"

"You're kidding. You mean he actually heard it's heart beating? Are you sure?"

"Of course, I'm sure, honey. I wouldn't tell you something like that if I weren't sure! It's true!"

"I can't wait to get home and hear it for myself then!"

At that precise moment, I didn't know whether to tell him the doctor had used a stethoscope or not; I assumed he would know that. He was so excited, however, that I didn't want to spoil his enthusiasm one bit.

When we arrived home, Johnny was dying to try to hear the baby's heartbeat. He knelt down beside the chair I was sitting in, leaned over, and placed his ear on my stomach. He listened intently for a few minutes then suddenly exclaimed, "I hear it, I hear it. This is unbelievable!"

"It's unbelievable all right," I thought to myself, "because it's impossible. I have no idea what he is hearing, but it can't be a heartbeat. He'd have to have a stethoscope." I was certainly not going to spoil the moment for anything in the world. While we were pondering this phenomenon, Johnny's ear pressed against my stomach as I sat in the chair, a thought came into my mind about another heartbeat at another time, at another place.

During the fall of my senior year, a group of us was riding around as usual, looking for something to do that would not get us in too much trouble but yet be fun. After riding around awhile, someone suggested, "Gary, let's just go to your house if it's okay and hang out in your basement."

"Sounds good to me," another said, "if it's all right with his folks."

"Okay, if you all are tired of riding around, then that's what we'll do, not much going on tonight anyway," Gary agreed.

Soon, some of us were dancing to "Rock around the Clock," a particular favorite of ours; some were shooting pool and generally having a pretty good time. However, the dancing and pool soon gave way to talk and gossip. It was mentioned that a teenage girl from a nearby town had created quite a stir by getting on the television show called *I've Got a Secret*. Guests would appear on the program with a special secret, and the celebrities, who appeared on the program regularly, would try to guess what their secret was. The girl's secret had been that her name was Mary Christmas. She and her parents had gotten a free trip to New York and had created a lot of excitement in their town.

"Let's think of something we could do to get on television," someone said.

"Gosh, yes, wouldn't that be a scream!" another chimed in.

We all got carried away with the idea of what a commotion that would cause in our little town and the attention we would receive from such an endeavor. We all set about thinking of what we could to do to merit the attention of *I've Got a Secret*.

After a great deal of animated discussion, we still had not come up with any brilliant ideas. It happened that Gary had been showing Nelson his father's new tape recorder. He had shown him how a person could record his voice and then play it back on this machine. We all became quite interested in recording our own voices and then playing the tape back. We would all ask the same question, "Do I really sound like that?" Gary would rewind the tape from one reel to the other, and we would start over.

"I've got it," Butch snapped his fingers. "Let's record someone's heartbeat and dance to it."

"That's it. That's great. They'll never guess that!" everyone agreed.

"We danced to a heartbeat; that's the secret!" Sara interjected. "But we all can't be on the program. What are we going to do?"

Everyone agreed that Butch and I should do the dancing since we were the ones who had a great routine for "Rock around the Clock." It was Gary's machine, or his father's, so it was decided that it should be his heartbeat. Now, exactly who would go to New York would be decided later. We then proceeded to record Gary's heartbeat with the microphone pressed against his chest. The volume was turned all the way up, and sure enough, it could be heard loud and clear. Butch and I then began a series of dance steps to the regular drone of Gary's heart. Neither the sound nor the rhythm ever changed; therefore, Butch and I tried to become more elaborate with our dance steps. I couldn't help but wonder, as we were dancing, what Daddy would think of this number if he thought "Over the Mountain, Across the Sea" sounded like a funeral. After about thirty minutes of dance maneuvers that Fred Astaire would have envied, someone finally pointed out that the dance mattered not one iota; no one would ever see it. After all, you just told them your secret; you did not demonstrate it. The joke was on us. We all ended up laughing hysterically and wound up in a heap on the floor. *I've Got a Secret* never heard from us, mercifully; therefore, the show would remain forever unaware of the entertainment it provided for a group of bored teenagers from Cherryville, North Carolina.

"Stop laughing, Brenda. You've got to be still so I can hear it," Johnny pleaded.

I didn't even try to tell Johnny why I had gotten tickled. I didn't think he would understand; it was really one of those situations where you had to be there to appreciate the humor.

"Let's face it, Johnny. We can't stay in this position all night with your head pressed against my stomach."

"What's so funny anyway?" he asked, somewhat disappointed.

"I was just thinking what an odd sight we would make if anyone could see us," and with that, he got up off the floor from beside the chair and got tickled himself.

"You're right. I guess we would look a little strange – but darn it, that's amazing" as he kissed me affectionately on the cheek.

"Yes, it's truly amazing," I thought as I kissed him back and got up to prepare supper.

#####

EISENHOWER

My letters to home were now filled with details of all kinds, describing what the baby was doing. Now that our families knew about the baby and were obviously as happy as we were, I could not tell them enough about the activity that was taking place inside my body. I wrote vivid descriptions of exactly what I perceived the baby to be doing.

"Today, I felt him at two different places at once," I wrote. "He must have legs and hands moving around at the same time.

"It thrills Johnny and me when the baby moves. We can now even see it moving! Isn't that amazing!" I went on to say. "One side of me has a big lump at times while the other side is sunk in; then all of a sudden, that side rises and the other side subsides. It's like the waves far out in the ocean, swiftly rising to a crest, and then receding again to meet the ocean, a constant motion of ups and downs, back and forth. That's what this baby reminds me of – the ocean. He's constantly in motion." Sometimes we referred to the baby as "he," other times "she." However, most of the time, it was referred to as "he," whether we were consciously aware of this or not. The doctor informed me this was either a "darn big baby," or I was further along than they thought. It was exciting that I may be further along; in spite of how much I was enjoying being pregnant, I simply could not wait to welcome this new little somebody into our lives.

We had heard President Eisenhower's speech on the radio that he made on March 16. I had listened to it again when it was rebroadcast the following morning. I was really concerned for my baby's future, and by the time Johnny had gotten home that night, I was in a tizzy.

"Johnny, the world's in a critical and tense time, according to the president's speech. I've never really thought much about things like this before, but now, everything's changed so, us here and all." "Now, Brenda, don't you get upset about Ike's speech; he knows what he's doing."

"Do you think the Russians will attack America?"

"No, honey, there's no way they would attack us. Khrushchev is a big bag of wind," Johnny tried to assure me.

"But, Johnny, Dulles said ten years ago that Russia's goal is to dominate the world and that they'd stop at nothing!"

"Brenda, Brenda, do you not know that we'll stop at nothing to stop them! Now, honey, I'm telling you, that's what the president is going to do. He's going to meet with Khrushchev, and they're going to talk all this out at a summit meeting."

"I don't understand this political stuff, and it upsets me something awful! What's this summit thing, anyway?"

"It's when the top leaders of the superpowers of the world meet and have a conference about the issues in the world." He went on soothingly, "As long as the leaders are talking – that's the main thing – there won't be war, you can rest assured of that."

"It scares me to death, all this talk of moving dependents out of Berlin. I couldn't bear to be without you when the baby comes."

I began sobbing.

"Now, now, honey, the army is just looking out for the wives and children of its soldiers; we wouldn't want or expect any less."

"Do you think they'll evacuate us?"

"I know we soldiers will stay here. That's our job – to keep the peace – but I can tell you this for sure: if there's any hint of danger, I'd want you and the other dependents out of harm's way. The army would see that you got out, and I would want them to."

Johnny finally managed to convince me that we were all safe and secure for now and that everything would be fine. He felt that once Khrushchev and the president met, there would be no chance of us being separated and that world conditions would be more stable.

At least now, the visions I had of bombs flying and civilization being destroyed had been alleviated. Just living in a place where a war had so recently destroyed and affected so many lives was one of the reasons all of these foreboding thoughts were uppermost in my mind, I felt.

Monsieur Roche had recently taken Johnny on a tour of the once secret tunnels and chambers that were directly beneath where we were living. Monsieur Roche had revealed to Johnny that he and his family, friends, and neighbors had dug those tunnels when it had become evident that the Germans were going to invade. They had worked furiously in an attempt to provide hiding places for themselves. The tunnels were of such length that one of them was the distance of about seventy-five to a hundred yards, where it finally came to an end. It opened up in a wooded area where, Monsieur Roche explained, that if need be, they planned to escape by this route. However, the entire village had been occupied by the Germans and the tunnels discovered. In addition, the German officers had used monsieur's house as a headquarters, keeping he and his wife confined to one area. He felt fortunate, however, that he was still alive to tell the story. His wife had died of a heart attack not long after the Germans had pulled out and the war had ended.

I had found this story to be both disturbing and frightening. We had moved from Madam Cassier's whose house had been broken into by the Germans and her husband whisked away, evidently, to his death. Now, here we were, living just above secret passageways, which had been intended for use to escape from the Germans. It was an ominous feeling! I prayed to God that those tunnels would never ever need to be used for their original intent but, instead, would remain forever a haven for Monsieur Roche's bottles of wine!

#####

MAYBELLENE

Johnny was elated with his birthday present, and it was definitely a surprise! He had no idea in the world that his little stay-at-home wife would manage to get a motorbike for him. With Papa's help, I had done it! Johnny was twenty-two years old on March 22. I thought it ironic when I considered the fact that I had celebrated my nineteenth birthday on October 19, five months earlier; my sister, Laurean, had become a teenager on March 13 of 1959; and now Johnny was twenty-two on the twenty-second. Somewhere in all that, I felt there had to be some symbolic meaning, but I could not figure it out. It was interesting, however, and I reflected upon it often once I was aware of the fact.

I could not resist climbing on the back of the bike and going for a quick ride with him.

"Brenda, hold on tight even though I'm not going very fast," Johnny warned.

"Go as fast as you want to. I won't fall off, I promise," determined that I was going to ride that motorbike.

"Okay, but be careful, honey. Hold on!"

Johnny started pedaling as fast as he could; then he released the clutch, and the motor started. Away we went! I loved riding on the back, but I wanted to ride it myself – all by myself. We rode down the street, whizzing past the stone walls, the fields, the houses, and on through the village. I had that same feeling of exhilaration I had experienced when I rode with Nikki.

"Now, it's my turn," I said as we slowed down, entering the compound.

"Wait a minute, Brenda. I don't know if you should do that or not!"

"I'm not an idiot, Johnny. I'm not going to let anything happen to this baby, you know that. I want to ride by myself!" I said determinedly.

"You be careful, Brenda. You go slow; you will, won't you?" Johnny asked, seeming to have some doubts as to whether I would or not.

"Of course, I'll go slow. Show me again how to start this thing," I demanded impatiently.

Johnny reluctantly let go of the handlebars and handed the bike over to me. "Watch for cars, now."

I was soon on my way, my hair blowing in the wind, my maternity top billowing around me, zipping past the landscape of the outskirts of Saint-Jean de Bray.

I was enjoying myself to the utmost and was returning home when I spotted Mama beside the road in front of her house. She must have seen me when I passed by the first time. She was signaling me to stop. It was obvious she was upset.

"Ce n'est pas bon pour bebe!" she fussed. I knew good and well she was reprimanding me for riding the bike in my condition, but I pretended not to understand. She was lecturing away in rapid French and, at the same time, gesturing toward my stomach and then toward the bike. I gave her a queried look and then quickly kissed her on the cheeks, pointed to my watch as if I had to hurry and leave, and sped off with a jerk. Mama just buried her face in her hands in dismay. I made a mental note to simply not pass Mama and Papa's house when I was riding a motorbike. I would go the long way around just to avoid Mama's admonitions.

As I accelerated to pass a French farmer and his wagon full of hay, my mind reflected upon another time when I had been speeding, and someone had tried to stop me. I was in my 1948 Plymouth *Maybellene*. My car, *Maybellene*, had been named for the hit tune "Maybellene" that had been popular about the same time that I had gotten my car for my sixteenth birthday. The incident of which I was thinking had taken place one night after we had been practicing for a high-school play. As I was one of the few cast members to have a car, I offered to take some of the others home. Two of the guys, who needed a ride, happened to be seniors, and being a sophomore, I wanted to make an impression on them. Now, to make an impression, I thought, would be to take them on a ride they would not soon forget. I would show them I was both exciting and daring, what more would one want in a girl?

There was a long stretch of road, right outside of town, called Old Post that many young drivers tried just such feats. I headed for this road with my soon-to-be impressed passengers. When the guys saw I was building up my speed, they asked me to slow down politely. Then they began pleading as they saw the needle on the speedometer move up to sixty, seventy miles per hour.

"Hey, girl, you could get us killed!" yelled one. I do not know what got into me that night. I had never done anything quite that foolish, at least behind the wheel of a car, in my life. It seemed as though an inner force was driving me on, and I pushed the gas pedal harder.

"She's scaring the hell out of me," said one to the other and then to me. "Slow down, Brenda. This isn't funny," pleaded my senior friend.

By this time, I was carried by an emotion I could not explain and went even faster. As we sped down the hill, the boy, who was in the back, crouched down in the back floorboard behind the front seats. The other one was in the floorboard of the front. We swooped to the bottom of the hill and started climbing the next. It was only then that I let up on the gas. We had gotten up to ninety miles an hour in that old 1948 Plymouth! *Maybellene* had been true that night! By golly, I was impressed! As to whether I had impressed them, I could only guess. I never saw them again, except during rehearsals on the stage, and they never again seemed to need a ride home afterward.

As I rode through the compound gates, I looked up at the blue sky above and thanked God that he had been with us that potentially disastrous night. I thanked him that he had let me live long enough to marry Johnny, come to this place, and have a baby. While kicking the kickstand down in order to hold the motorbike up, however, I could not help but wonder how it might have felt to have raced, just once, in one of those powder-puff derbies.

#####

Torn

We had received a disturbing letter from home concerning my father's health. Johnny's father and mine, as well, had suffered heart attacks in the year preceding our wedding. We were always concerned about the health of those at home but especially these two.

We were told that Daddy had had some kind of spell while working in the yard. He was taken to the hospital by ambulance. Mother assured us that it sounded much worse than it really was and that everything was all right now. In fact, it had not been his heart at all but some type of stomach disorder, which had caused the pain. I could not help but wonder, however, if these were false assurances in order to allay our fears.

How I loved and adored my father. We had a special and unique relationship. Perhaps one reason he was especially close to me was that their first baby, a little girl, had been stillborn. Exactly one year and one day later, I had been born. I was over two months premature, and they had nearly lost me also. I had been told that I was kept in an incubator a month, and then was still so tiny when I was brought home that a doll bed was used for me to sleep in.

I was torn with mixed emotions. I yearned to see and be near my father, to help care for him and assure myself that he was all right. The part of me that was a wife and having a baby knew that I had to be with Johnny. We simply had to be together when the baby was born. I consoled myself with the thought that Daddy had mother, Laurean, sisters, brothers, and friends to care and be with him while Johnny had only me.

128

Paris

"Spring was a beautiful, uplifting season anywhere in the world," I imagined, "but spring in France had to be the most beautiful." There were flowers of all kinds everywhere in Orleans. That was probably the reason I had been somewhat disappointed when we had visited Paris the previous Sunday. I had been surprised that many of the elaborate fountains throughout the city were not even turned on. "The person who wrote the song 'April in Paris' certainly was not inspired by how things appeared on that particular Sunday in April of 1959," I thought.

It had been quite exciting going to the top of the Eiffel Tower, however. I could simply not imagine anyone building such a monstrosity of a structure as this. We were informed that Alexander Gustave Eiffel had designed and built the tower for the exposition of 1889. We were astonished to learn that restaurants were on several of the platforms of the tower. The tower itself provided a breathtaking sight of Paris as the city spread in all directions far below us.

It frightened me a little being up so high, but I was captivated by the fact that I – Brenda Stroupe, a young girl from a little town in the United States – was actually looking out over Paris from the Eiffel Tower.

I also could not imagine why anyone would turn a trip down to sightsee in Paris, either. Johnny and I had invited Bridgie and Vince to ride with us that day. Bridgie wanted to come, but Vince said he could see all of Paris that he wanted to in the movies.

"Where is your spirit of adventure, Vince?" I asked.

"I can get all the adventure I want sitting right here on my couch, Brenda," he had replied.

"You're going to miss a marvelous trip, and Johnny will do the driving. You'll have a chauffeur, Vince, you won't even have to bother with the traffic," I implored, but there was no way of budging Vince once his mind was made up.

While we were riding around Paris, we happened to cross over a bridge, which spanned the Seine River. As we reached the middle of the bridge, I screamed so loud that Johnny narrowly missed hitting a motorbike rider who was just in front of us.

"For crying out loud, Brenda, don't do that to me! It's hard enough driving without you screaming!"

"But, Johnny, look, look quick. It's the Statue of Liberty, and it's here on this bridge!"

"Honey, it's the Statue of Liberty all right, but for gosh sakes, look how small it is! You're going to get us killed, yelling and carrying on like that every time you see something!"

"Well, my gosh, Johnny, who would have ever thought the Statue of Liberty would have suddenly appeared right in front of our eyes here in France!" I responded, hurt that he had not shared the same astonishment that I had.

"You know that the French gave the Statue of Liberty to the United States, don't you, Brenda?"

"Of course, I know that. I just didn't know there was another one. That really took me by surprise, that's all," I replied, feeling slightly annoyed.

We parked the car and walked for a little while after that. We sat down at one of the many sidewalk cafes to enjoy the scenery, the music, and the people passing by. I loved to order since I knew how to say, "I would like a ham sandwich and a Coca-Cola" in French. That is the only thing we ever ordered, however, since that was all I knew how to say. Johnny said he wished I would learn how to say something else; he was tired of ham sandwiches, but I smartly retorted that, at least, I could say that much, and that was more than he could do.

"That'll pay him back for yelling at me on the bridge," I thought to myself as I turned my attention to the waiter.

I adored how the waiters opened Coca-Cola bottles. It was worth everything it costs just to witness that.

The waiter would swing the bottle ceremoniously between his legs and hold the bottle there in position with his legs pressed tightly as he "popped" the cap off the bottles. He then served it to you with a flourish! It was pure art.

"Oh, aren't these Frenchmen grand?" I thought. "They can even make serving a Coke sexy!"

#####

WEIGHT WATCHER

Mother had written us that some of her friends and mine were going to give me a baby shower there at home and then send the presents to us. I could not imagine that anyone could possibly care about us that much to spend time and effort having a baby shower and us not even there. I just cried when I read that letter.

"That's about the nicest thing I've ever heard," Johnny stated upon hearing about it.

"Can you believe they are doing that for us?" I said.

"No, but again, I say it's the nicest thing I can think of, and we are two very lucky people to have friends at home who care that much," Johnny answered with his usual wisdom.

"Oh, and I can't wait to get that box from the States, won't that be exciting! I hope they do it soon so I'll know what to buy and what not to buy for the baby!" I continued, mainly talking to myself for Johnny was now getting his materials out to start painting.

Johnny and I had enjoyed so much the art displays on the sidewalks of Paris that we had become inspired to try painting ourselves. We decided that each of us would paint something for the baby. After all, the French were known for their art. It would be a paint-by-number painting but a painting just the same. I had decided to paint the picture of a cocker spaniel as I had had one most of the years I was growing up. His name was Toby, and I had loved him dearly. Johnny decided on a picture of two bird dogs, a pointer and a setter, for he had had two just like that while growing up. He had spent many happy hours hunting with them. We were limited in our choices just what to paint as dogs was the only category the paintings came in. The PX was always limited on its merchandise. We thought that perhaps some day the baby may appreciate our efforts, even if he or she could not right away. Besides, it gave us something constructive to do with our time while waiting upon its arrival.

We were quite proud of our efforts toward preparing for the baby. I had taken an old army pillowcase and made the baby a little laundry bag. I embroidered "B-A-B-Y" on it and put a drawstring through the top. I also tore up an army sheet and made baby sheets for the bassinet. I hemmed the edges by hand.

In addition to the bassinet Johnny had brought home, he brought in a bathinet some time after that. It was a pretty neat contraption. One could fill it with water and use it to give the baby a bath in, and then empty the water by way of a hose underneath. A padded top folded down over the bathing part, which then became a dressing area for the baby. When finished, the entire apparatus could be folded and put away. I was extremely thankful for the latter feature as our little rooms were getting fairly crowded with all sorts of paraphernalia.

I was having a difficult time watching my weight. I had three doctors, and each one of them would lecture me about my weight on each visit.

The doctor came into the examining room where I was waiting and said, "Mrs. Stroupe, you have done it again!" I practically trembled underneath my sheet. I was so afraid they were going to put me in the hospital for my weight problem.

"But I did what you said. I followed the diet," I said, knowing it sounded false but, in fact, was the truth.

"We told you that you could gain three pounds, and you gained six! We don't know what we're going to do with you!"

He gave me a twelve-hundred calorie diet and instructed me to come the following Friday. It was not just the weight factor he wanted to check, but my blood was low also.

I left that office determined to follow his instructions to the letter. I was so upset that they may take me away from Johnny and put me in the hospital that I swore I would not eat from Tuesday until Friday, when I was to go back. I would show them why, they would be begging me to gain a little weight.

On Friday, the WAC nurse who was weighing me screamed out loud, threw down her pencil, and actually ran into the doctor's office, proclaiming, "This girl has gained five pounds since Tuesday! She's actually gained five pounds in three days!"

I was so humiliated. I had tried so hard not to gain and then to be treated like that. She did not have to make such a production of it! I reacted in the only manner a person in this situation would: I cried.

Thank goodness, the doctor believed me. He sat down and explained a lot of things to me about salt and liquid in the body. He went on to explain the dangers of gaining too much weight. The army had set the weight limit at twenty pounds, and I was almost there. I told him I understood that, but I could not help I had gained. He gave me some pills to help me lose and assured me they were watching out for me and would take care of me. The good news was that my blood was normal. At least he was kind to me. I was to go back in four days.

"Don't let any of this bother you," I wrote our families. "By this you can tell that they are keeping a close tab on the baby and me. I have all the faith and trust in my doctors in the world; it's those WAC nurses I don't like. They just gloat when I've gained weight and make snide remarks to me," I continued.

"You know what I think, Johnny Stroupe?" There was no reply because he knew I would tell him anyway. "I think those WACs are jealous. They know they're so ugly and act so hateful that no one would want to have a baby with them, that's what I think."

"Brenda, honey, don't let them upset you. We have everything going for us; we're experiencing the biggest thrill of our lives. Let's not let a few nurses spoil it for us" as he pulled me over to him and got as close to me as he could.

Just at that precise moment, with my stomach pressed against Johnny, the baby kicked so hard that it jolted us. We began laughing out loud. It was just as though the baby had said, "Don't leave me out of anything you two."

"We have the smartest baby in the world," Johnny exclaimed, his face still flushed from laughing.

"I'll say we do, Johnny. He's already so smart. I hate to think how smart he'll be when he's born."

And so it went, the two of us making the best of things in those two little rooms and making the most of every sign of life the unborn baby emitted. We could not wait until this little person would become a part of our lives. Nothing could possibly burst the bubble of happiness in which Johnny and I had surrounded ourselves.

#####

THE PARADE

Orleans was a city buzzing with activity. The biggest holiday of the year was just around the corner, and everything had to be just right to pay homage to the maid of Orleans, Saint Joan of Arc. She was the heroine of Orleans.

The excitement and anticipation was contagious as all kinds of celebrations were being planned in honor of her. I wanted to know more about this courageous young girl and how it was that she had come to lead an army. Johnny brought me a book from the post library about her.

I, of course, had heard of Joan of Arc. I had, at least, an inkling of her accomplishments. She had been very young, I knew, and she had led soldiers in battle. I vaguely recalled something about visions and her hearing God speak to her. That was about the extent of my knowledge of this young maid.

The more I read of this young girl, the more enthralled I became with her story, her life, and the absolute saintliness of her. No wonder she was the national heroine of France! I found myself feeling somewhat honored that she was referred to as the maid of Orleans, for now, at least I had ties to the city.

What a tremendous testimony her life was! If people would only read about Joan of Arc (Jeanne d' Arc) and believe it to be true, they would know that God had indeed led this young girl.

I tried to imagine the courage, the bravery, the sheer fortitude it must have taken for a fifteen-year-old to gain an audience with the Dauphin (rightful heir to the throne of France) and declare to him that she not only was sent by God to save the city of Orleans from the English but to bring him, the Dauphin, to be crowned king! With a sign that no one could have possibly have known, other than by divine intervention, Joan convinced Charles VII that she was ordained by God and her mission divine. But others had to be convinced. In Pointiers, Joan was examined by clergy of the university at great length to determine if, indeed, her voices came from God. Finally, they were satisfied. Then it had to be established for a fact that she was a female, for some had rumored that she was a boy. It had to be proven that she was not only female but a virgin as well. In the fifteenth century, it was strongly believed that nothing evil could be emitted through a virgin.

All this in itself would make one back down, I would think, and go home. But she persevered. Her mission was clear to her, and she would let nothing deter her from the course God had set her on. I just had to take a deep breath and put the book down. If she had done no more than all this, she had demonstrated a profound faith beyond ordinary human understanding.

Orleans had been under siege by the English since October of the previous year when Joan led her troops into the city during April of 1429. After days of battle, assault after assault upon the English with her leading the troops, even planting the first scaling ladder against the strong stone walls, the English turned their backs and ran.

Miraculously, Joan had predicted her own injury – an arrow struck her above the right breast – and indeed, it had as she was attempting to place that first ladder.

By the time I had read the story of Joan of Arc, I, like the French all around us, could not wait for the celebrations! I felt I could now grasp the significance of this girl upon these people and this land.

Johnny and I mingled with thousands upon thousands of people on that warm day in May of 1959 in the heart of Orleans to see Joan of Arc come riding into the city on a white horse, carrying the banner of France. The girl, who rode upon that horse, was quite young, or so it appeared. How this girl's heart must have been beating to have been chosen the "one" to represent the national heroine. I felt confident her life would forever be affected by this day. And then – much to our surprise – we saw Charles de Gaulle standing tall in the back of an open car, waving to the people! The crowd pressed closer and tighter, screaming with excitement.

"Johnny, Johnny get his picture – quick try!" I screamed. "He'll be by in a second."

"I can't see, but I'll try." Then I watched as Johnny held the camera high over his head and, without being able to see, snapped a picture.

To both our amazement and delight, several days later, we developed a perfect picture of Charles de Gaulle, president of France.

Do As The French Do

We began doing some of the same things that the French people did for recreation and leisure. We began to avoid going to the caserne as much and began imitating the French. We started picnicking almost every Sunday. We observed how family oriented they appeared as they played with their children in the many parks that dotted the city. They especially liked to float little toy boats in the water or play ball with the children. We would spread a blanket out right on the grass and enjoy the outdoors, watching families having fun together. Sometimes Sue and Dee and their little boy would join us, or Pete and his latest girlfriend would go with us.

We went to a large exhibition of camping equipment in Orleans one Sunday afternoon. We noticed that the French were very much into camping. We found the tents and camping paraphernalia quite interesting and discussed keeping this in mind for our family in the future.

On the days Johnny did not ride the motorbike to work, I would ride it to the bakery and get French bread. I would strap the long loaf – unwrapped – on the back of my bike and ride home just like the French. I loved just breaking it off and eating it with butter. I always remembered to go around Mama's, however, as I did not want to be the recipient of a scolding.

Johnny, on some days, would put our dirty laundry in a laundry bag and strap it on the back of the bike and drive it to work with him. He made a funny sight, in his soldier's uniform, perched on that bike with the bulky laundry bag behind him. No one thought anything of it, though, as they were doing the same. We were certainly saving by using the motorbike when we could. The oddest thing I noted was mothers on a motorbike pulling baby carriages behind them. I wondered if I would do that when the baby came.

"No, I think not," I thought. "One must draw the line somewhere," and I wondered what folks back home would think or do if they ever saw me doing such a thing as that.

#####

THE FATHERS

Johnny's father, Garland, had written us the cutest letter. It was somewhat a rarity to hear from him anyway, so this letter was extra special. He was so proud that he would soon be a grandpa again. Johnny's older sister had a little girl of two. If he preferred a boy or a girl, he did not say, just that he would be very proud. He said that he would love to see little Brenda or perhaps he should say big Brenda now.

He had been helping Jerry, Johnny's older brother, at the soda shop and seemed to be really enjoying it. He had retired from his job at the textile plant due to his heart attack, so this gave him something to occupy his time.

He went on to tell us how he had been caught by the game warden with two undersized walleyed pike, which had cost him twelve dollars. He really did not mind, though, he said, as he just thought of all the times he had not been caught.

He wrote, "Your buddy Mike has been here twice since he got married. He and his bride had been to Florida on their honeymoon and stopped by on their way back to New York. Mike and I had a few shots of white lightning together to celebrate."

Whether they were celebrating Mike's marriage or the fact that we were having a baby, he never made clear. He even told us there was a song called "White Lightning," and he played it on the jukebox at the soda shop every chance he got.

He mentioned my father's recent illness but assured me that he was fine. He wished us luck and blessed us at the end of his letter.

"Your father is a character, Johnny. I can't wait to get to know him better. I hope we can all be close."

"He's a character, all right, and so is yours. Remember the stunt they pulled after our wedding?"

"Remember, I don't think anyone will ever forget. I'm glad we were on our honeymoon. They said your mother had a fit she was so mad at him."

"You really can't blame her now, can you, Brenda? Wouldn't you be mad at me?"

"But, Johnny, it is funny; you've got to see the humor in it, and besides, it'll be something we can tell our grandchildren."

Johnny began to smile and said, "Wouldn't you have liked to have been a fly on the wall when my dad didn't get home from our wedding until the day after? There he was, still in his white dinner jacket, it filthy dirty and ripped up the back."

"And your mother asked him how in the world he had managed to do that, and he said it got snagged on a barbed-wire fence!" By this time, I was laughing so hard it was hurting my sides. I was holding my stomach with both hands.

Johnny picked up from there. "Then mother asked him where in the hell he'd run into barbed wire, and he told her he didn't know; he was just following your dad, Russ!" By this time, we were both gasping for breath; we were so tickled as we tried to imagine where our fathers had been for over twenty-four hours after our wedding ceremony. Evidently, Garland had been trying to console my father who was taking things pretty hard after Johnny and I left. He and Garland went off together, and no one saw them again until the next day.

"One thing is for certain: they enjoy each other's company!" said Johnny.

"You know, those two could be dangerous together; we'll have to watch them real close when we get home!"

"You can say that again!"

#####

OVERALLS

The last week of May brought Johnny and me a most wonderful surprise. The box containing the baby-shower gifts arrived! It had taken twenty-four days to get to France, which was exceptionally good timing, especially considering the size of the box. I do not know who was more excited – Johnny or me? While he began unpacking the box, I ran all around the compound, gathering anyone I could find to come and be a part of our spontaneous baby shower. By the time I returned, I had an appreciable group of children and adults behind me.

Johnny had some of the gifts already lying out on the bed. Some were wrapped, and others were not. I spotted among the infant gowns and receiving blankets a Dr. Spock book! "Just what I needed," I thought and picked it up. There inside the cover was an inscription. "For my niece or nephew, with all my love, Aunt Lolly," and then she had added a personal note to me. "Brenda, I went uptown and picked this out all by myself."

My little sister, how I missed her. "She's growing up, and I'm missing it," I thought as I began eagerly opening another gift.

There, lying in the bottom of the box, carefully folded was a little pair of overalls. I just could not help but start crying as I picked up the little Osh Kosh overalls! Everyone, including Johnny, looked at me for an explanation. I was clutching the little denim overalls close to my chest as tears trickled down my cheeks. I proceeded to try to convey to all of them the significance of these special miniature overalls.

"When my mother was expecting their first baby, my father spotted these little overalls in a store window. They were being used as an advertisement for Osh Kosh merchandise. He was so captivated by them that he approached the manager of the store about buying them. 'No, there was no way those could be sold,' the man informed him. 'They were solely for advertising purposes.' But my father persisted until finally, he came out of the store with those little overalls, complete with a set of miniature tools in the back pocket.

"Upon his arrival home, he presented the overalls to mother and said that perhaps with the help of them, the Boggs could get a boy in the family to carry on the name. He informed her that these little overalls would accompany them to the hospital and hang by her side when the baby was to be born.

"They had done just that. When the time came, however, the outcome had been an unfortunate one. The baby, a little girl, was stillborn. Their hearts were broken.

"The little overalls saw them through this tragic episode and were carefully packed away to wait upon the arrival of, hopefully, another baby at another time.

"Exactly one day and one year later, I was born two months premature and clung precariously to life. The little overalls were still hanging by my mother as the two of them rejoiced at my birth and prayed that I would make it. One month later, when my parents proudly brought me home, the little overalls were still with them. There would be another time, God willing, and they would hang yet again.

"For years afterward, the overalls were passed to my father's brothers and sisters when they were having their babies. Of all the babies born from that time on, however, only two were boys, but the little overalls remained an essential part of the birthing process."

Now it was our time. How touched I was at this moment to think that Daddy had remembered to send them. Oh yes, and they would be hanging beside me when I went to have the baby, that was certain!

Everyone enjoyed the story and looked at the overalls in a slightly different way. They were handled with the utmost care, as if they were a special prize.

We laid everything out on the bed for a proper display. They all ooed and ahhed as each little gown, each set of booties, diaper sets, and assorted blankets and baby goods were opened. We were delighted our neighbors and friends seemed to share our excitement and joy of this occasion with us. They all knew what it meant to be remembered by those at home; they had all experienced these moments from time to time and were more than glad to share this special occasion with us.

After everyone had left, Johnny and I kept looking at each item, trying to imagine what it would be like when we really had a baby to put them on. We were up until midnight, carefully putting everything away and reading each letter of best wishes and congratulations for the baby to-be.

"Johnny, wasn't that a nice comment Captain Tanner's wife made?"

"What was that, hon? A lot of nice things were said."

"You know, about her never having seen anybody from home doing so much for someone overseas. She thought it was real touching."

"I'm a little surprised she came at all, being a captain's wife! They, the officers, don't usually have much to do with us peons, you know."

"Oh, Johnny, they're people just like we are; they have feelings just as we do."

"You just don't understand the army, do you, honey? The army doesn't think people are people; there's ones like us on the bottom, and everyone else is above us, the ones who really count."

"We really count, Johnny Stroupe. I've never felt any other way. You're no. 1, as far as I'm concerned."

"My paycheck would prove you wrong, dear, but I'm glad you think that way. I'll say one thing. I bet no officer in the army has as many things for a baby as we do right now."

"That's the truth; I've got to try to figure out a place to keep all these things and still have room for a baby."

Later, after we had gotten in bed, I kept talking about all the nice gifts we had received from home, how kind the people had been for doing all this for us, and how sweet the letters were. Thank-you notes would simply not be enough. I would write each person a long letter I vowed.

It was then I realized Johnny was sound asleep and not hearing a word I was saying.

I said out loud, knowing he couldn't hear, "You may be a spec four to the army, but to the baby and me, you're a commander in chief, Johnny Stroupe."

#####

THE SALE

The size of our living quarters was beginning to be a real concern of ours. The two little rooms that we had spent so many happy hours the past few months in began to take on a different appearance when we considered there would soon be three of us instead of two. A baby would be small, that was true, but a baby did require certain essentials that would take up some space.

Johnny and I began to pack away and put in a big box any of our clothes that were not absolutely essential. We were simply going to send them home in order to provide the space we needed so desperately. Then, a remarkable thing occurred.

Simone and Alice dropped by one afternoon as I was sorting out which items of clothing to keep and which ones to send home.

"Brenda, if you really don't think you'll use these clothes again, I think I have an idea," Simone said with her French accent I loved so.

"No, Simone, I really don't think I'll ever be able to even get in these again" as I held up a pair of very tiny-looking shorts; I replied as I thought to myself that I had actually been wearing these eight months ago.

"Well, I have some friends that would die to buy some American-made clothes. Would you mind if I sent them over?"

"No, I guess not. Well, I just have never thought of selling my clothes. Is that what you mean?"

"Oh yes, and Johnny's too that he may not want," Simone replied excitedly.

I contemplated this idea for a few minutes. It had never occurred to me to try to sell my clothes, but the more I thought about it, the better I liked the idea.

"I'll talk to Johnny when he gets home tonight," I said, "and if he agrees, we're in business!"

Alice said, "You mean you'll sell your clothes, Brenda?"

"If we're not going to use them again, it's really a good idea. We get them out of the way, get a little something from them, and don't even have to bother with all that boxing and mailing them home!"

It was evident that Alice was fairly amused but picked up on the excitement as Simone and I continued talking,

"If Johnny agrees, Simone, we'll give you a portion of the money, all right?"

"Okay. That would be good for all of us, right?"

"Right," I replied, getting more excited all the time. When Johnny got home that evening, there was really never a discussion; my mind was made up.

The next few days brought a flurry of activity to our little place. Simone must have contacted everyone working for Americans in the area, or otherwise, about the clothes! For some reason, the French boys and girls loved these clothes from America. It was unbelievable; I was getting as much as four dollars for Johnny's used cotton plaid shirts! Everything was sold in a matter of days – everything – including some things we had not originally planned on selling. Johnny and I even began trying to find items of clothing we just thought we may have wanted to get rid of. We even sold the few civilian ties that he had. "I felt a little guilty, but they seemed so happy to get them," I thought. Maybe we were doing them a favor.

"Boy, Brenda, I'm glad you sent all that stuff over here now. This is really great! Not only did we get those things out of the way but we made a real good profit!"

I was pretty pleased with myself, and Simone was thrilled too! Alice was still a little in disbelief as she simply could not imagine selling one's own clothes. However, she lived with her mother and father in a big house with plenty of space, and too, her father was a colonel.

#####

Wait, Weight

Johnny and I began seriously looking for another place to live. We would look on the weekends, but the apartments we saw were either filthy, or the rent was as much as sixty to eighty dollars a month! We simply could not afford it. We would not give up, we vowed, and we could wait until after the baby was born if we had to.

I was seeing the doctors weekly now. It seemed to me that all they were concerned about was my weight, and all I was concerned with was having the baby. We were confused as to when the baby was due. One doctor would say I was further along than they thought, and it could be as early as the last of May. Then another would say that it appeared more like the end of June. It kept Johnny and me in constant perplexity as to just when to look for this baby.

I had devised my own plan for keeping my weight down. My appointments were every Tuesday, so from Sunday morning until after my appointment on Tuesday afternoon, I would eat nothing but boiled eggs. As soon as we left the doctor's office, Johnny would then take me downstairs to the snack bar where I would indulge myself with a scrumptious banana split. The plan worked!

"Mrs. Stroupe, we're pleased with the efforts you've made toward maintaining your weight. If you can stay at about this, 126, and not gain much more, you'll be out of the woods," Captain Griffith stated proudly. "This baby could possibly be here by month's end."

As this was May 19, I become quite excited just thinking of the possibility of being a mother by June. I could not wait to have this baby for more than just the ordinary reasons. I had become to dread these doctor's appointments. The thought of any of them reprimanding me for something I could not help upset me terribly. The constant threat of being put in the hospital for my weight problem had scared me to death. Not that I was afraid of the hospital, but I could not stand the thought of being separated from Johnny. This possibility had been like a cloud hanging over us for about a month; therefore, I was greatly relieved to think that the baby would soon be here, and that problem would be dissolved.

The baby, who was quite active, had now begun to hurt at times with the strong movements.

"Our baby has them all beat," I wrote my parents. "He doesn't just move around in there, I could declare that he stands up and takes a walk."

Arrangements were being written back and forth across the Atlantic as to just how Johnny would relay the news to our parents.

It was decided that Johnny would call instead of sending a cable. We, therefore, warned them not to be upset if they got a phone call during the night or in the wee hours of the morning.

We informed them that we had everything ready for the baby. The little overalls were even packed in my suitcase with my gowns and other necessities. We had decided to use our middle names for the baby's middle name whether it was a boy of girl: Franklin or Louise. We still were not sure of the first names.

We sat back and waited and waited and then waited some more. We finished our paintings of the dogs and then set about doing photograph albums. We titled one album "Homesick" and filled it with pictures, which had been sent to us from home. We titled the other one "Our Life in France," which contained the pictures we had made since being here. We had developed most of these ourselves and were quite proud of that fact.

I dreaded to see Tuesdays come. I was so hoping I would be having a baby before I would have to keep that appointment and step on those scales. By now, though, I had really lost my appetite, but I continued to be extremely nervous about being weighed.

As the month of June began to pass and still no baby, I became increasingly depressed and despondent, which was highly unusual for me. I pulled the curtains over the french doors in the daytime, hoping to discourage visitors. Everyone was concerned and would drop by to see if "anything had happened." Of course, it had not, and that only made me feel worse. I no longer felt like writing, and Johnny found himself with pen in hand, writing to the folks back home.

"Thought I would drop a line and let you know the little family hasn't forgotten you. Brenda is doing fine but has just not been in a writing mood lately. We keep thinking that, surely, the baby will come today or tomorrow and that you will be getting a telephone call before a letter could reach you. The doctor has told us now the baby may be a week or two late, so please don't worry."

He went on to tell them that the fellows in the finance office had bets on which day the baby would come. They had all lost their bets as the days they had guessed passed and no baby.

Somehow, this did not make me feel any better. I personally felt betting on the birth of a baby was inappropriate. I would not have expressed this to Johnny; but I, secretly, was glad they had lost, Johnny included as he had bet too.

Johnny closed by telling them he hoped they would be hearing his voice before they received this letter.

CELEBRATE

Sunday night, June 28, just before midnight, my back felt like someone was driving swords into it. I felt like this was going to be it but hesitated to wake Johnny quite yet. There was no pain at all in the abdominal area as I would have thought there would be, so I decided to wait. I dozed off and on between these stabbinglike pains in my back, and then, at five in the morning, a sharp pain jolted me awake. Johnny woke up to my squeezing his arm. He became fully awake when he realized what was happening. We hugged each other and became quite excited as we began to time the pains. They were coming less than five minutes apart! As we had not had a telephone since being in France, we simply had to remember what the doctor had said and decided on our own as to when to go to the hospital. We were each trying to stay calm for the other.

The pains would stop for a while and then start again. By nine, we decided it was time to leave. As we were getting ready, Coreen came running out to the car and started crying.

The old chateau, which had been converted into a hospital, was at La Chapel, Saint-Mesmin, about twenty miles away. We made the drive with the little overalls in my lap.

As soon as we got to the hospital, I was whisked to the maternity ward where I received immediate attention. The girls attending me were French, and I managed to speak enough French to them for a few exchanges. One commented that she had never seen anyone so happy to be in labor; I understood that much.

I was put in a hospital bed in a small room and was given some paper to write down the time of my pains. The little overalls were hung up at the top of my bed. As I was fairly comfortable between pains, I decided to use the paper to write my family. Now that the birth was imminent, I felt like writing and bringing them up-to-date on the past few hours.

One of the men had come from Johnny's office during that time to tell him that my family had placed a call to Johnny at the office. I couldn't believe it! They had called just at the time I was going to the hospital. We had not written for a while, and they had become concerned.

"Oh no, now they will worry about me," I thought. "Will they know I'm here in the hospital? What were they told?"

The doctor assured Johnny that the baby would not be born until late that evening more than likely. Johnny was advised that the best thing he could do would be to go back to the office and wait on my parents to call. I agreed with this; that way, we could inform them that everything was all right. Johnny, however, refused to leave the hospital but, instead, sent a message with a friend.

I was given some soup to eat, orange juice, milk, and water. The pains were still sporadic, and so I continued to write home. It was better than just lying there, and it helped me feel close to them by putting my thoughts in writing. Johnny was in the waiting area right outside the door; they would only allow him to come in occasionally.

There I was, by myself, happily writing away there in the labor room.

"So far, I don't know what is to come, of course, but it hasn't been that bad at all. Maybe it's because I'm so happy that the baby finally decided to come."

I continued to write after the nurses had checked on me again.

"My prayers are for this baby. The main thing is for it to be healthy and normal. We could not ask for anything more than that."

Now, feeling vulnerable that time was drawing near, I made a confession, "You know, it makes no difference to us really if it is a boy or girl. I know I promised Daddy a boy, but if Johnny loves a little girl like my Daddy has loved me, I wouldn't want her to miss out on that for anything. Now, all that I can think about is how much I want this baby to make it."

This was true. I could not help but think of what had happened to my would-have-been older sister; I prayed with all my heart and soul.

"God, if it be your will, let this baby be normal and healthy. Please don't let anything happen to it. God, I'm a little scared. I know I can't hide that from you, but don't let anyone see this. Help me be brave, please. Be with the doctors and nurses, be with Johnny, be with us both as we all bring this little life into the world."

Johnny had refused to leave the hospital. He had insisted on staying right outside my door, in the hall. The only thing Johnny had to sit on was the radiator, which, of course, was not being used as it was the end of June. Dee, Sue's husband, worked in the dental department downstairs. Once he realized we were there, he made regular checks on Johnny.

By Monday night, the baby had not made its appearance. Doctors and nurses were constantly checking on me. In direct contrast to the nurses at the office, these were as nice and as sweet as could be. I knew they were doing everything they could to help me.

Captain Pearson came in to talk with Johnny and me. They both stood beside my bed.

"Sometimes a first baby can take a while getting into the world," he assured us. "Everything is fine. We'll just have to be patient."

The bars had been raised on the sides of the bed; this was for my protection, I was informed, so that I would not accidentally fall out. I was given a sleeping pill so that, hopefully, I could rest between pains.

"You need the rest, Brenda. The baby will probably be born in the morning sometime."

"I hope so, Captain Pearson, for all our sakes. Our parents are aware I'm at the hospital, so they're waiting on a call." I then turned to Johnny. "Johnny, where are you going to be? Where are you going to sleep?"

"Don't worry about me, sweetheart. I'll be right out here in the hall, right outside your door; they won't let me stay in here with you."

The next twenty-four hours became a blur. The pains became sharper and grew more intense. They seemed to last longer, come sooner, and hurt more. I remember vaguely asking for something for pain and was told it would only slow up the birthing process. Could I possibly make it? and I told them that I could. Johnny would be in and out. I would squeeze his hand and then attempt to sit up so that he could hold me. He would then be sent out of the room.

At some point on Tuesday night, Captain Silverman and Captain Griffith came in and examined me. Captain Griffith then said matter-of-factly, "Mrs. Stroupe, you have us puzzled."

Fear went through my body. "If I have them puzzled, then I must be in trouble," I thought hazily.

"We are sending you down for x-rays so that we can get a better idea of what is happening."

"I know what's happening," I thought. "I'm dying, and you're not telling me; the pain is so bad I must be dying. God let my baby live!"

"Johnny, Johnny take care of the baby. Promise me you'll take care of the baby!" I was screaming but did not realize it.

"Can you please give her something for pain?" Johnny implored later. "Can't you do something!"

"We're doing all we can, son. The baby is big, and it's going to take time. The x-rays indicate that it is too far down in the birth canal to do a cesarean; we've got to wait it out."

People were in and out of the room constantly, it seemed. I was given liquids, and aids would wipe my face with damp cloths and wet my lips with mineral oil.

By this time, I was speaking French to the WACs and English to the French aids. I was incoherent. Now, I did not even try to be polite and ask for something for pain. I lost all dignity and literally begged!

"Kimberly, Johnny. Name her Kimberly Louise if I don't make it – I'm dying, I know I am; tell me the truth – Hold me, Johnny, hold me. Tell everyone at home how much I love them."

Just when I thought I could stand no more, I was taken to the delivery room. Someone over me said soothingly, "It's time, Brenda. We're taking you to delivery; it won't be long now."

"Don't push, Brenda, not now. The doctor will be here in just a minute, don't push! I see the crown!"

"Don't push. What does she mean 'the crown'? Does that mean the crown of its head? God, help me!" I felt I was falling into a horrendous big black hole. I was falling and would never come back.

I found out later that this nurse was to have been off duty at two o'clock but refused to leave my side. She would stay, she had declared, until that girl had this baby.

"It's a boy, Brenda. It's a boy and a good-size one at that!" Captain Pearson held him up for me to see. I looked at the most beautiful sight in all the world. A perfect baby!

"I'll be darn," Captain Pearson exclaimed, "if those little overalls didn't work!" It wasn't until then I noticed that they were hanging from the end of a cart for carrying instruments. Captain Pearson winked at me. "We knew you wouldn't want to be without them!"

I managed a smile and asked weakly, "Is he all right? Is he all right?"

"Ten fingers and ten toes. Looks all right to me," Captain Pearson replied. The nurse carried him over to the scales. "Eight pounds and fourteen ounces. What is his name to be?"

"Terry," I replied. "Terry Franklin."

"Oh, surely you're going to name him Terrance and call him Terry."

"No, it's Terry. That's what my husband wanted his name to be, and Terry it is."

I couldn't believe it was over. I simply could not believe it. "Thank you, God. Thank you for our baby!"

I was whisked out on the stretcher with baby in my arms to meet his daddy. Johnny kissed me on the forehead and then on my dry, parched lips right there in front of everybody.

"He looks just like me, Brenda. He looks just like me, doesn't he?"

"He sure does, darling. He sure does. Now please hurry! Go make that call. I know they are all dying at home!"

#####

HOMECOMING

I awoke from a sound sleep with three smiling doctors looking down at me. They were Captain Griffith, Captain Pearson, and Captain Silverman. They had been truly concerned for me during the labor. They explained to me why they had not wanted to give me something for pain. It would have affected the baby and made the labor even longer. I told them everything was fine now. I was just glad it was all over. They said they were too.

We were the proudest and happiest couple in the world. No two people could be any happier. We finally had our baby in our arms, and all three of us were fine. Johnny swore he had ridge prints on his bottom from sitting on that radiator so long. But other than that, we were all in real good shape.

The next few days were busy ones for me. I was breast-feeding every four hours, walking the halls to get my strength back, and trying to rest in between feedings and taking walks. The babies were kept in the nursery until feeding time and then were brought to the mothers.

Johnny read me the letter he had written the families before he mailed it. In order that the families know every detail, I felt I must write just in case Johnny had omitted something. "You left some things out," I said to Johnny. "I don't write a book like you, honey. Nobody writes letters like you.

"He's the biggest baby in the nursery," I didn't tell them there were only four babies in there; that was beside the point. I described him as being the exact image of Johnny.

"I can't find a thing on him that looks like me, except for perhaps his bowlegs. He has little long fingers, little long feet with little long toes like Johnny's," I wrote. I am confident people could tell I was deliriously happy, writing descriptions like that. We joined the ranks of many other first-time parents, I am sure, becoming slightly giddy over the birth of a baby.

"He's the king of the nursery too. The nurses adore him. They refer to him as Paul Bunyan, Little Hamburger, Little Man – all kinds of nicknames. They think he's just precious, which he is!"

We found out later that the workers in the hospital would pass one another in the hall and ask if the young girl upstairs had had the baby yet. We also learned that the story of the overalls had gotten around. Some people actually came by my room to see the overalls, which tickled me to death.

One afternoon, as Johnny was coming in to visit me, he was surprised to find me sitting up in bed with the silk sash used to tie my housecoat around my chest.

"What in the world are you doing, Brenda?"

"I'm measuring my bust size," I said quite proudly.

Since Terry had been born and I had begun nursing, I had become fascinated with the transformation in my breasts! I felt they were enormous. Being slightly over a hundred pounds when I married, this was a phenomenon to which I was completely unaccustomed.

"Do I have a surprise for you! I have the same bust size as Bridget Bardo!" I announced.

"My gosh, Brenda, don't let anyone hear you. What in the world would make you think about such a thing?"

"I don't know. I just thought it would be fun to compare." Johnny was somewhat flabbergasted and, to my amusement, seemed a little embarrassed.

"How do you know that?" he asked.

"I measured with this silk sash, and then I took it down the hall to the stand-up scales where they weigh and measure you, and I measured it on that, that's how!"

"Oh lord, Brenda, what will you think of next? Please don't tell anyone; that's so personal – will you please!"

"Of course not, Johnny. You know I wouldn't tell anyone but you – something like that!"

I could not wait to write the girls at home about this amazing statistic! By golly, they would know how to appreciate it!

It was one week after Terry's birth that we finally got to bring him home. The doctors were watching me closely; they told us that I was close to being given a blood transfusion.

"Wednesday, July 8, was the most exciting, most wonderful, and happiest day of my life," I wrote home. "We brought Terry home!

"It is almost a sin to be this happy," I wrote to my mother.

THE BUBBLE BURST

It had been wonderful getting back to our little house again. The words "Be it ever so humble, there's no place like home" came into my mind from a song. I had been in the hospital a total of ten days but had seemed even longer. We had come home on a Wednesday. Johnny had that day and the next off and was to return to work on Friday. We experienced almost two full days of complete bliss, rejoicing in the fact the Terry was now with us and sharing our life.

"Forever, Johnny. Just think forever. We'll be a family, our own little boy."

"He'll be a good boy, Brenda. I know that he will because we'll be the best parents we know how to be."

We would stand over the bassinet and look down at him. We just wished that all the folks back home could see him. How proud they would be of him and how happy it would make them to see the three of us together.

Johnny left for work Friday morning, July 10. He kissed me as I lay in bed, waiting for Terry to wake up for his next feeding. He leaned down and kissed Terry in his bassinet, which was at the foot of our bed. He eased the french door open and closed it softly behind him as he left.

Terry woke up at about eight o'clock to be fed. After he went back to sleep, I got dressed and was straightening up when I heard a car pull up. There was a pounding on the door and someone yelling something. I could not tell who it was but opened the door immediately. It was Johnny! Before I could react to the surprise of seeing him back so soon, he all but knocked me down, falling into my arms and sobbing out loud.

"Johnny, Johnny, what is it? What's happened? What's wrong?" I screamed. I was terrified. He was crying profusely. He was in such turmoil he could not get the words out but managed to stammer, "Dad . . . Dad . . . dead . . . dead!" Realizing that Johnny referred to my father as "Dad," I was panic-stricken.

"Who, Johnny? Who . . . whose dad?" For minutes that seemed like hours, I was paralyzed with fear, not wanting it to be either one, praying it was not one of ours – hoping against hope – something had gone drastically wrong, and I had not heard the word "dead."

"Johnny, please . . . please . . . tell me who is dead. Which one, Johnny, which one – yours or mine?"

Finally, I could make out the words, "Mine . . . mine . . . my dad is dead!"

Now that I knew, it was just as horrible as if it had been my own. A sickening feeling – overtaking my body, indicating death – finally reached my head, and the realization of what Johnny was trying to say made its impact.

"No, Johnny, no. There's no death, no one's dead. It's a horrible, horrible mistake, that's all. You'll see, you'll see" as I grabbed him, and he pulled me down with him to the floor where we both collapsed. We lay in each other's arms there on the floor, sobbing our hearts out. I do not know how long we stayed like this, but by the time I got up, I knew it must be true. Johnny was in such a state that I knew it had to be true. He had to know for sure. "He would not have upset me like this. He would not have interrupted our life in such a way if he did not know it to be true"; my mind was thinking crazily.

I tried to pull him up from the floor. "Please, Johnny, get up. Please tell me what has happened," I implored.

Little Terry had slept through all this, unaware that he had lost a grandfather, one he would never know or see. He had lost a grandfather that would never see him either, a grandfather that had just learned less than a week ago that he had a grandson.

When Johnny was able, he told me that after he had been at work for about an hour, the Red Cross had called him. It seems they had been trying to locate Johnny since Wednesday, the day we had brought Terry home, to inform him of his father's death. They were holding the body back home, waiting on a response from Johnny as to whether he could come or not. He knew no other details concerning his father's death.

"Of course, you must go, darling, you must go. You have to be with your family!" I stated emphatically.

"I can't leave you, Brenda. I just can't, not you and the baby by yourselves."

"What did the Red Cross say? What did they tell you to do?" I asked unsteadily.

"We're to give them an answer by lunch. I've got to get back to the office to call."

"I'm going with you, Johnny. The baby and I are going with you."

"Let me run and tell someone where we're going and what's happened," I said. I found Coreen at the clothesline. When I told her what had happened, she assured me that they would look after me while Johnny was gone. "I knew that. That's why I told him he must go, Coreen."

Once inside the finance office at the post, I began to feel that this was indeed happening; it was not a bad dream. The others were trying to console us and expressing sympathy. Some just did not know what to do or say, so they made over Terry. A French girl, who was working in the office, took Terry in her arms. He slept contentedly in her arms as I sat next to Johnny and his commanding officer as they tried to make arrangements for Johnny to go home.

In the end, it was just not feasible. We were told the army could fly him home definitely right now, but he would have to come back by ship. That was the best they could do.

I knew if it were my father Johnny would understand that I simply must go, and I felt the same for him.

Johnny steadfastly refused to go if they could not guarantee his return in two weeks. There was no way they could do that. It would be thirty days or nothing at all.

"Then I can't go. I would consider leaving her and the baby maybe ten days, fourteen at the most, but not a month!"

My heart went out to Johnny as he gave his consent to inform the Red Cross to let his family know that he would not be coming home for the funeral; they could now carry on with the service.

It was with heavy hearts that we left the office around lunch on Friday. Just forty-eight hours earlier, we had been on top of the world, experiencing the joy of a lifetime, and now, we were grief-stricken.

We went back home for the second time within two days, this time with a much different feeling from the exhilaration we had felt earlier. We were numb. We did not talk on the drive home. We were occupied with our private feelings. I was feeling guilty for keeping Johnny from going home, and Johnny was torn between his heart's desire to be with his family at home and that of his responsibility toward the baby and me.

Terry, our darling little baby, oblivious to all of this, gave more meaning to our lives than ever before. Because of him, we would get through this – we had to; we were his mother and dad.

God's Watchful Eye

The next few days were a blur. We were not only in a state of shock we were in the depths of despair, whether we realized it or not. Everyone had come by to offer us any kind of assistance they possibly could give us, but there was nothing anyone could do. We were in mourning; but there was no body, there were no wreaths, there was no pastor to offer us any kind of comfort, and there was no service to attend. The worst part of all was that we only had each other to hug and console; not another human being that was there with us, well intended as they might be, even knew Johnny's father. They could only imagine how we may feel, they could sympathize; but we had not one other person, except for each other, whose shoulder we could truly cry on, each suffering for the other. We were the only two who had known and loved the person personally for whom we were grieving.

As much as I felt for Johnny, I truly could only empathize as I was thinking how I would feel if it were my dad. I really had not gotten to know Garland real well. Johnny and I had had a relatively short courtship and were engaged only six weeks. I had simply not had the time to develop a relationship with him.

The neighbors brought dishes of food for us of which we could hardly eat. Bridgie and Vince came and visited and expressed sympathy and related how Vince had lost his father as a young man. Coreen and Roy hovered over us. The ones from the finance office came by with flowers from the ones at Johnny's work. Sue and Dee were continually checking on us, and of course, there was Mama and Papa. Even monsieur, in his stiff way, appeared sad as he went about his chores around the compound.

When the French children came, carrying flowers in their hands, I thought my heart would break. They felt so sad for us, they said, and then turned their attention toward the baby. No matter what state of mind a person is in, a baby can always lift the spirits. After all, a baby's needs had to be fulfilled, no matter what was going on in the world around him.

They looked at Terry lying in his bassinet, all their little heads peering over the sides to get as close a look as possible. I lifted Terry out of his bed and told them all to sit down. Then one by one, I handed him to each one. They examined all of his tiny features: his nose, his chin, his little hands and feet. They held him and marveled over him so gently that even Johnny smiled.

Johnny was eager to hear some of the details regarding his father's death. Somehow, we felt that may help in some way. We assumed it was a heart attack since he had had one previously, and we were unaware of him being sick. Of course, we surmised they may have kept something from us with the impending birth of the baby and all. We could only guess as to what may have happened and where and how.

It was a full week before we received any tangible evidence that this tragedy had indeed occurred. Johnny brought home several sympathy cards from work and a poignant letter from my mother. She described how Johnny's father, Garland, had been out riding by himself toward the mountains near Morganton. It was his forty-seventh birthday, and he wanted to just ride, as was his custom, and to see some of his friends. He had pulled the car off the side of the road beside a field in order to greet one of his friends. As he got out of the car, he waved and yelled to him. He then fell beside the car, dying instantly. She went on to tell us how Johnny's mother, Naomi, had called her (my mother) to come to the house quick, that Garland was dying somewhere up the road, and she (Naomi) did not have a car.

We learned later that Johnny's younger sister, Janice, had been talking on the phone when the operator had interrupted and told them to hang up and wait on an emergency call. Janice had yelled for Johnny's mother, and when the phone rang, Janice had picked it up to hear the words, "Are you Garland's daughter? Well, he's dead!" Janice had dropped the phone in shock. Naomi then spoke to the person on the other end. The word "ambulance" was mentioned, so this had indicated to Naomi that he must be alive and not dead as Janice had heard. She and Janice then frantically began calling people, trying to find a car.

By the time my mother had gotten to Johnny's house, Naomi and Janice – along with Johnny's older brother, Jerry – had already left and were on their way to Morganton.

When Naomi and family arrived at the site, there was nothing more to do but identify the body. Mother had stayed at Naomi's and was there, anxiously waiting when the distraught group returned.

Now, we knew some details. At least he had not suffered, we comforted ourselves. He had had a good day and was doing exactly what he enjoyed most: rambling about the countryside, meeting and talking farm talk with friends.

In the days following, we received lengthy letters from both of Johnny's sisters. They went into great detail about the days spent waiting to hear from Johnny, then finally the service. They even sent pictures of the many flowers that had been sent to the funeral.

My heart especially ached for Janice, hearing the news of her father in such an abrupt way. It was similar to the way in which Johnny had heard. I supposed there was no gentle way, however, to become aware of such a loss.

I stayed by Johnny's side and watched over him the best I could. I would do anything to get him through this difficult time.

In the meantime, we had our precious little Terry to think about, sleeping away in his bassinet. He made absolutely no demands except to be fed and changed.

Bridgie asked me one day, "Brenda, what is the formula for having such a good baby? He sleeps all the time."

"There's no formula, Bridgie. You just have to have Terry! You know, Bridgie, I believe if that baby would look up at Johnny and me and say, 'I want the world,' we'd break our necks, trying to get it for him," I said jokingly.

"There's nothing like being a parent," she replied.

"Johnny is wonderful about helping me with him. You should see Johnny give him a bath in the bassinet. It's hilarious! I pretend I'm busy in the kitchen but keep peeping around the corner of the door to spy on him!"

"That's fantastic, Brenda. Why, Vince didn't hold ours until they were three months old!"

"Terry has been a blessing for us in more ways than one. Since Johnny heard about his dad, he and Terry are practically inseparable. He just holds him tight against him, and I can tell that he's thinking about his dad."

"You know it's been difficult for him, Brenda, but I feel for you too."

"We're doing the best we can, Bridgie. We're doing the only thing we know to do: go on." Johnny has a strong faith, and that is seeing him through. God is watching over us, all three of us, we truly believe that.

#####

MOTHER

Mama came in with a note from Papa. The note explained that they had found us an apartment in uptown Orleans if we were interested. He went on to say in the note that they would regret not having us nearby but knew we were terribly crowded.

As apartments were extremely difficult to find for those of us unauthorized, I practically squeezed Mama to death. Only the French themselves could make these kinds of connections, and they had done it.

"Oh, Mama, you know I'll miss being near you, but look, we're practically bursting at the seams!"

She replied amiably, even though I could only grasp a word here and there, but the important thing was we both understood.

Suddenly, having Mama there with me made me feel terribly sad. I wanted to see my own mother so much that I almost began to cry. There were so many things I wanted to ask her advice about concerning Terry and personal things about myself too. I had so many questions I needed answered that only a mother and daughter could discuss.

Mama was making over Terry; I knew she felt he was special to her too. After all, it was Mama who had proclaimed out loud there was to be a baby before anyone else would admit it. No matter how much she cared for him, however, we could not communicate enough for me to ask her the many personal things I needed to know. I felt a lump come into my throat, and tears welled in my eyes as I looked at her and Terry. How I yearned for his own grandmothers to be able to do just this, hold him in their arms and smother him with love.

"Oh, Mama, Mama," I thought, "I love you, but I need my mother," and somehow, I knew that if Mama were aware of my thoughts, she would understand.

#####

ORLEANS

Johnny, Terry, and I left our wonderful friends at the compound on August 1. Terry was one month old. Mama and Papa had done it again! With the connections that sometimes only the locals could make, they had found for us what we thought to be a wonderful apartment in the city of Orleans. We lived directly on the street in an upstairs apartment overlooking the Loire River.

We now had four entire rooms of our very own! We had a good-size kitchen, which contained a large stove and a refrigerator. There was a nice-size dining room furnished with an ornate carved dining set: a table, six chairs, and a huge china cupboard. This would serve as our den. There was a large bedroom, which contained a bed, dresser, and a large wardrobe. The windows of the bedroom opened to the street. The fourth room, which was really a foyer, made a perfect nursery for Terry. The door used for an entrance opened into this room; but it was just the right size for a baby's crib, which we had bought from the Com-z Exchange Shop; the bassinet, which we could leave up now to use as a changing table; and a chest of drawers for Terry's little baby clothes and other essentials. We were also thrilled that we had an inside toilet of sorts. Not that our families at home would consider it a bathroom, but for us, nonetheless, a bathroom. It consisted of a tiny enclosed area with a cement floor. The cement had a hole directly in the center of it with an impression on either side of the hole, indicative of the position in which one should place his feet in order to make use of the facility. A cord hung on the back wall, which would flush when pulled. It was a big improvement over the outdoor one we had used at monsieur's.

Johnny and I were delighted with our new living arrangements. We could finally spread out, which was indeed a luxury.

From my kitchen window, I could observe the goings on of the street. People were continuously passing by, shopping, riding their motorbikes, and going about their business. I would open the shutters completely so that I too could feel a part of the outside. I could see in the distance the huge bridge that crossed the Loire River leading into Orleans. We had been told it was the only bridge left intact after the war; all the others had been bombed. It was said that a total of thirty thousand cars passed over this bridge each day, sometimes causing tremendous traffic jams.

I found it amusing too that I could watch my dish water, after I had opened the drain, run right out into the gutter beside the sidewalk. I would watch from the window for the soapsuds and water to appear just below me shortly after it made its way down the drain through the pipes and then directly onto the street.

There was a city ordinance about the side of the street on which we parked our cars. We had to rotate the parking of our car every other day. On Mondays, Wednesdays, and Fridays, all the cars parked on the left side of the street, on the other days cars were parked on the right side. This made for an easier traffic flow as the streets were quite narrow. It was also essential for street cleaning. There was a strict fine for anyone who violated this law. Like everyone else, Johnny brought the motorbike inside with him at night. All bicycles and motorbikes were off the streets at night. After all, for the majority of people, the bicycles and motorbikes was their only means of transportation. To have one stolen would have been a major catastrophe.

Johnny came home one evening not long after we moved with a wonderful surprise.

"Johnny, it's a cute little thing, but what is it?" I asked, really not knowing.

"It's a washing machine, Brenda, a washing machine! Now, you won't have to wash diapers by hand!"

"That little contraption is a washing machine!" I stared incredulously at what looked to be a huge pot with a dome-type lid on it. I could not help but get tickled and held my hand over my mouth, trying to stifle the giggles. I would never intentionally hurt Johnny's feelings, but this was preposterous.

"Now, wait a minute. Just let me show you how it works" as he eagerly set about demonstrating it.

He then proceeded to show me that the dome lid contained a motor. When plugged in and locked in position over the container underneath, it really did agitate and wash the clothes.

"It's called a dormitory washing machine," he explained. "These little machines are actually advertised for students away at college to wash a few personal items in."

"What do I do? Pour the water in it to wash, then pour it out to rinse, and so on?"

"Yeah, that's about how it works, but it's better than doing it in a dishpan, isn't it?" He wanted me to share his enthusiasm obviously.

"You're right about that, honey. That will be a tremendous help."

Washing diapers and keeping them ready for Terry was a monumental task. As we had no hot water, I had to heat the water on the stove first. I rinsed the diapers four times after they were washed so that there would be no soap residue on them. It was a fairly lengthy procedure, but I did not want my baby's little bottom to have a rash on my account. They were usually dried on the wooden stand-up rack inside, or occasionally, I would hang them outside on the clotheslines provided for the apartments. It rained so often that it was necessary to have clotheslines with a cover over them, which, of course, meant the clothes received no direct sunlight. To me, there was no advantage of hanging them out.

Our little house again became a center of activity, now that we had more space. Two of the new men from Johnny's office – Troy and Jack, who had both just recently come from the States to the finance office – came over about two nights a week to play canasta with us. We did not mind it at all and, in fact, looked forward to their coming. I would work especially hard on those days to have the apartment nice and straight; have Terry bathed, his little clothes and diapers all washed and put up; and have supper ready as soon as Johnny came in.

Sometimes Troy and Jack would send word that they were coming early and would prepare the evening meal for all of us. The kitchen would be turned over to them, and they would dare me to come in. I especially looked forward to these occasions as it was a real treat. Johnny and I both took it as a compliment that so many people seemed to feel at home there and made a habit of dropping by. We knew it provided a homelike atmosphere for the single guys, a change from the barrack life. Pete continued to dote on Terry and even gave us ten dollars to put in his piggy bank. Now that we were closer to the post and because of the baby, many of the ones from the office dropped by fairly often.

SERENADE

One night, in the middle of August, as Johnny and I were preparing to go to bed, we heard a commotion outside. The noise caught our attention right away as the streets were relatively quiet after dark. As we were considering what this might be, to our surprise, we heard the strains of "Carolina Moon" being sung in English.

Johnny said, "Oh no" and went straight to the window, unlatched, and opened the shutters. Below the window, singing away, were several young soldiers from Johnny's company being directed by Pete, who appeared slightly intoxicated, in song. "Brenda, come over to the window; they're serenading you."

As I was putting on a robe and straightening my hair, I looked at Johnny for an explanation.

"Hurry, come to the window," he said, offering none.

I just looked down at them sweetly, having no idea what this was about as they continued singing.

As they started to leave, Johnny yelled down and asked them to come up. They told him they could not and for us to just have a good night.

"What in the world was that about, Johnny? It was sweet of them, but why?"

"It's like this, honey. You had your six weeks checkup today, and they know it."

"What . . . what!" I said as I could feel my face beginning to burn with embarrassment. "You mean they came here and sang because they know that . . . they know that . . ." I could not even finish.

"That's horrible, Johnny. That's barbaric. I'm so embarrassed – I wish I had thrown something at them," I yelled.

"Honey, don't be upset. It's kind of a little ritual around here. They do it to everybody when the baby is six weeks old."

"Well, I certainly have not heard any of the other women mention anything about it," I snapped.

"They just probably didn't think about it. Honest, it's really flattering!"

"Flattering, my eye. I think it's disgusting. It's like everybody knows our business. Why, Johnny, how can I look at them!"

"For gosh sakes, honey, don't get upset. Please don't make so much of this. You know Pete wouldn't hurt your feelings for anything. It's their way of having a little fun; they probably wish they were married, if the truth were known."

"How did they know I was going today?" I asked brusquely.

"You know I had to get off work to take you and Terry to the doctor's office. Everyone in the office knows Terry's six weeks old, Brenda."

"All right, Johnny, but I tell you one thing. If I find out this hasn't been done to the other new mothers around here, both you and Pete have had it," I muttered, half mad and half tickled.

After the lights were out and Johnny was asleep, I could not help but think to myself how good it had made me feel while they were singing before I knew the reason. Oh well, I would never have the thrill of being serenaded at college by a fraternity. This was the closest I would ever come to that, so in retrospect, maybe it had been a real nice thing for them to do. I would try to think like that anyway as I turned over and went to sleep.

JOAN OF ARC

I would get the French baby carriage out that Mama had loaned me, put Terry in it, and out into the streets of Orleans we would go. It was delightful to be strolling with my baby and looking in the shop windows.

Nothing thrilled me anymore than when I would be the recipient of a "Bonjour, madam" and especially if the person would inquire as to the baby's age and name. My French was adequate enough that I could answer these few questions. My halting French and Southern accent was a dead giveaway that I was American, I knew, but I felt quite pleased with myself when I successfully completed such a conversation.

As I strolled Terry down the street, my mind reflected upon the past year. We were now living in our third place since I arrived in Orleans a year ago; I reminded myself that we must take Terry and visit Madam Cassier before we went back to the States. I recalled the wonder I had felt as I stepped through the doors of the train station into Orleans and the anticipation I felt about beginning a new life not only as a newlywed but in a foreign country as well. I remembered how I had prayed for God to give me a French friend. "Not only had he answered that prayer but had given me my own little Frenchman," I thought.

Now here I was, walking along, pushing this carriage, with God's most precious gift: a baby. God had certainly watched over both Johnny and me during Terry's birth. His hand had been there, guiding the doctors to make possible this little life. He had been with us through the shock of hearing of Garland's death and was with us as we grieved over the loss and the anguish we felt at being separated from family and friends back home during that time.

How ludicrous it seemed, in retrospect, that God had been punishing us with something as insignificant as a smoked-up house and a car that would not run. "These were simply minor inconveniences in the scheme of life," I now realized. Two things – birth and death, the beginning and the end – were what really mattered, and God had seen us through both.

I paused on one of the side streets in front of a small statue of Joan of Arc. She had been sculptured in her battle armor, her hands together in prayer, and her head bowed. Her helmet was resting at her feet. As I looked up at the statue, I could not help but think again about this young girl whose life had ended so tragically at the very age I was right now: nineteen. She never experienced the life of a normal teenager – whatever that might have been in the fifteenth century – never had a boyfriend or married, and, certainly, never had an opportunity to bring a new life into the world.

"God," I prayed earnestly, "grant to me just a small portion of this girl's determined spirit, the faith that she had in you, and her desire to do your will, and I should be a faithful follower of yours the rest of my life."

Baby Talk

Terry, naturally, was the center of mine and Johnny's universe. There had simply never been a baby like him; of that, we were certain. He was so cute, smart, and strong. It was obvious he was a beautiful baby, and we knew he was smart because he said coo so early.

"Look, Brenda. Look how tight he's holding on to my finger. The boy really has a grip."

Sure enough, Terry was lying on the bed with Johnny beside him. Terry's little fingers were holding Johnny's finger so tight that Terry's little knuckles were white.

"Let's give him a rattler and see if he can hold that!" I suggested.

We proceeded to put a baby rattler with a handle on it in Terry's hand.

"He can, he can. Look how he's holding on to that rattler. My gosh, he's only six weeks old!" Johnny exclaimed.

Terry's little eyes would study us intently as we put our faces close to his and make baby talk. He loved it, we knew, when we talked to him.

"Sue said the other day when she came by that he was the most alert and strongest baby she had ever seen at that age, Johnny."

"You've got to remember, Brenda, he had a head start. I truly believe he was over two weeks old when he got here," Johnny said teasing me.

"You're crazy, Johnny Stroupe. You know that he's just the smartest baby in the whole world, France at least," I said as I gave them each a kiss. "My two guys. They always said I was boy crazy, and I'll admit it I was and am crazy over the two of you!"

Johnny grabbed me playfully and pulled me down on the bed with him and Terry. We happily spent the next hour playing with and marveling over our son. "This little piggy went to market, this little piggy stayed at home," we played with his toes.

"I never knew it was so much fun having a baby," I exclaimed.

#####

Stealing Apples

One day, I heard the sound of a bicycle bell ringing repeatedly on the street below my kitchen window. I was holding Terry in my arms. I looked out to see Simone, astride her bicycle, ringing its bell and looking up at the window for a response.

"I'll be right down to let you in," I called out the window. "What a great surprise," I thought as I went down the steps, carrying Terry to unlock the main door to the street.

We kissed each other in the French manner and then proceeded up the steps leading to our apartment.

Simone explained that the reason she was alone was that Colonel and Mrs. Boyce would not permit Alice to ride her bicycle that far from home and in the city. I would have loved to have seen her, but I certainly understood. It was good having Simone, however, and I was extremely pleased to see her.

She had something for me, she said – a bag of green apples. She had remembered how last year at this time I had made such a fuss over the apples the French children brought me, and she thought this an excellent surprise. It most certainly was, and while looking at the apples as Simone busily began putting them in a bowl, my mind began to wander to another time and place where there were many, many green apples, an orchard full in fact.

Bang! Bang! went the gunshots. Ole man Grover was shooting that shotgun of his for all it was worth. About a dozen of us, enough to fill two cars at any rate, were plundering the apple orchard again for the third time in as many nights.

"Hit the ditch, everybody, hit the ditch; he's shooting like crazy!" someone yelled above the noise of the gunshots.

We all scattered out and crouched as low as possible in the ditch, which separated the road from the apple orchard.

"Man, he was ready and waiting on us this time," Gary said excitedly. "Keep low everybody and real still."

"Where are the rest of them, Gary? I can't see a thing; it's so dark I just jumped for cover!"

"Spread out all along here. Just hope he doesn't let the dogs out. *Shh, shh,* Brenda. Be quiet and don't make a move," Gary warned.

I was tingling with excitement and eager anticipation as to what was going to happen next. I was panting for breath as we had dashed through the orchard and jumped for cover. This was part of the fun, really. We knew that the risk we took about getting caught or getting shot was why we did it.

My breathing was rapid as I kept my ears listening intently for footsteps or worse, dogs. I could hear Gary breathing hard just beside me as he crouched, poised and ready to run at the slightest move. We had been doing this off and on for a while now. It was called apple picking. We would load our cars with stolen apples and then go throw them at any of our peers who happened not to be with us on that particular night. Likely victims were other teenagers out walking or riding in the open rear end of pickup trucks, which was often the case. When you hit someone, you had "scored" or "picked" an apple. There was no particular person or groups that were sought out to victimize. One might be throwing at a group one night that they might be riding around with the next.

Bang, bang. A round of shots went off again, and I nearly jumped out of my skin. I moved closer to Gary now, more than a little frightened but not wanting to admit it.

"Hey, you know, this may not be such a bad setup, if it weren't for that shooting," Gary teased as, by now, I was holding on to him for dear life.

"Darn it, Gary. I'm scared. Are we going to make a run for the car?"

"Not as long as you're holding on to me like this, we're not. Besides, I think he's shooting up in the air!"

I got tickled just thinking about it now. We did eventually make a break and get away, leaving only a couple behind. We would go back later and pick up the ones left hiding there, but what fun we had during the apple season!

Simone never realized how far away my thoughts had been as she was chattering away about her father and the little overalls. He had said that he had four daughters: Simone and three older ones. Two of his daughters had had two daughters each. He was now considering getting a miniature pair of overalls to hang up when Simone's sister had her next baby; maybe they would bring him a grandson. I told Simone I could not wait to write my father that he may be responsible for beginning a new French tradition as she and I laughed heartily together.

Simone could not hold and play with Terry enough. She amused him in every way she could think of: making faces, noises, and holding various toys in front of him. She delighted in the responses he made to her antics.

Then Simone grew solemn and told me she had some sad news. She told me she was going back home for good, that one of her brothers-in-law had found her a job there. She would miss the colonel, his wife, and Alice, but she knew that they would be leaving someday. She would miss us too, she said.

"Simone, we'll stay in touch. We'll get your address and write to you! We'll try to see you before we leave too," I tried to reassure her.

"Things are forever changing, Brenda, and especially here, it seems. American families of soldiers move in, and then they move out. They're here, they're gone, and you and Johnny will leave too."

"We can't wait to get back home, Simone, you know that. I'm so homesick, just as you have been at times, but we'll never forget you, I promise you that."

We embraced and cried and promised each other we would stay in touch, write, and visit before we left, but deep down, we both knew we were saying good-bye forever. I filled her little basket with my most precious possession: bottles of Coca-Cola. I knew she loved them as much as I did. I then waved good-bye to her until she was out of sight.

#####

ANTICIPATION

The longing for home was becoming acute for Johnny and me. We no longer tried to spare the other one's feelings; we openly admitted and discussed how homesick we were. We wanted those at home to be able to see Terry and watch him grow as we were doing. Johnny had been so concerned about his younger sister, Janice, and his mother, the two of them at home, now alone. He yearned to be a comfort to them and help them in whatever way he could.

In spite of the ever-increasing desire to get home, however, our thoughts turned to travel. Both our families had encouraged us to travel, and realizing we may never have this opportunity again, we began making plans for a trip. Now that Terry was almost two months old, we felt he was a good age for traveling. We had been told that it was easier to travel with an infant than it would be later on.

Johnny had a real close friend from home who was stationed in Furth, Germany. He and his wife were both from our hometown. Even though I only knew Duck Jarrett and his wife, Mary Alma, slightly, I was elated with the prospect of seeing someone from home. It would be the next best thing to being there, talking to people who were from the same town. They had attended the same high school, hung out at the same places, and done the same things we had, more than likely.

Johnny came in from work one evening all excited.

"Guess what, guess what – have I got news for you!"

I fairly jumped up and down with excitement as I could not wait to hear what it was. Johnny was so excited he could not wait until we were settled down, as we usually did, but just blurted out as he came in the door.

"I talked to Duck Jarrett today in Germany! I finally found him, and you know what?"

"What? What?"

"They want us to come to Germany! They are feeling the same way we are and are just as anxious to see us as we are to see them. He insisted we stay with them a few days!"

"Oh, Johnny, this is wonderful. It's just too good! My gosh, we've got a lot of plans to make and things to do, haven't we?" I said as I began looking around and wondering what all it would entail to take Terry on such a trip, not to mention our clothes and things we would need.

Johnny continued, "He asked me our plans. I told him it had been a childhood dream of yours to go to Switzerland, and we were definitely going there."

"Oh, did you, Johnny? That was so sweet of you to say that to him."

Since I had read the book *Heidi*, as a little girl, I had always dreamed of going to Switzerland. I thought it to be the coziest thing imaginable to be tucked away somewhere high in the Swiss Alps, living by yourself with just your grandfather, eating cheese, and tending goats.

It was with great expectancy and excitement that we set about making plans to be gone the first two weeks of September. We would be traveling for fourteen whole days, covering Switzerland, Austria, and Germany. Johnny laid the map out on the table to plan our route. I could not believe it. I was going to Switzerland, the little country of my dreams.

"Johnny, did you know that Switzerland is the safest possible place that we could be if a war broke out?"

"How do you figure that, honey?" as he was studying and making notes on a sheet of paper beside the map.

"It's neutral. Switzerland is the one country that can never be in war because it refuses to take sides with anyone. Don't you find it interesting that the whole world can agree upon one thing: to leave Switzerland alone in time of war so that there will always be one place the enemies can meet and talk?" I informed Johnny as I folded diapers.

"Well, it may not be too neutral if a big bomb were dropped on it, I tell you that," Johnny flatly pronounced.

"Oh, but nobody would ever do that because all the nations have agreed, Johnny."

"Brenda, you amaze me. Sometimes you are so gullible. You mean you really believe that if someone like Hitler, for instance, ever got in control again, he would honor that promise?"

"Well, yes because that's how it is!"

"Whew, Brenda, it's a shame the whole world does not share your honesty and trustworthiness," he teased.

"You know, the Red Cross designed their flag based on Switzerland's flag because the Red Cross was founded there." I continued, "Switzerland's flag is red background with a white cross, so the Red Cross just reversed that." I felt sure this would convince Johnny that somehow Switzerland was guaranteed protection from all sides in the event of another world war.

Johnny never swayed with his opinion but did what any wise husband does when caught in a situation of this type: create a diversion.

"Did you get that button sewed on my khaki shirt today by any chance?" he inquired. "I need it tomorrow."

"I certainly did," proud that I had taken care of that little task before he had to remind me again, "and I also got your ties pressed. You're all ready for inspection.

"Wasn't I the clever one?" I thought. "I would stay ahead of him with these little tasks, and he would perhaps brag about me at the office," I thought as I stacked Terry's diapers in neat stacks and put them away in the drawers. "He didn't think I'd have that button sewed on. I just know he didn't" and turned my attention to the diapers in the pail.

#####

Narrow Escape

We crossed the Switzerland border late one dreary, rainy night. Terry was sleeping soundly in his car bed in the backseat. I could hardly wait for the border patrol to let us pass through the inspection area. Johnny was showing them our credentials and answering their questions quite patiently. I just wanted to scream, "Let us in, fellows. I've waited all my life to get here!" It was magnificent! The next day found us driving all over Geneva. We were charmed by the beauty of the place. Everywhere, everything was spotlessly clean, so different from France. The huge flowered patterns and designs formed with thousands of many-colored flowers in the sides of the banks fascinated us. The fountain in the middle of the lake formed a beautiful arch, appearing a mile in height, there in the center of the lake. Brightly colored sails billowing in the wind, with Mont Blanc in the background, gave the entire scene a majestic touch. We crossed the Mont Blanc Bridge with flags representing nations all around the world, flying from each side of the bridge.

As much as we had to watch our budget, we were determined to have one thing, if nothing else: a Swiss cuckoo clock, and that, we did! We purchased a clock from a clock store right there in the heart of Geneva. Oh how I wished we could get one for everybody at home. The clocks were an amazement themselves. There were cuckoo clocks of every kind and description imaginable. They played music on the hour and the half hour. They had little Swiss-attired figures popping in and out on the hour and yodeling. There were elaborate ones, there were simpler ones, but they all were delightful! We looked and looked at the clocks and watches until Terry started crying, and we had to go back to the car.

The following day found us in Zurich, Switzerland's largest city. We were more impressed than we had been the day before with the cleanliness and neatness of that city. A few people, in native costume, were there on the sidewalk, yodeling. The unusual sound of the yodelers was spellbinding. We stopped and listened for sometime. This made me think fondly again of my favorite book, *Heidi*, the little orphan girl who had found happiness with her grandfather in the Swiss Alps. What a wonderful childhood memory for me, and now to think, I had visited the country of my childhood dreams.

"Well, Brenda, was Switzerland everything you thought it would be?" Johnny asked as we were preparing to leave.

"Oh yes, yes and more! Thank you, darling. Thank you so much for bringing me here!" Looking down at Terry, I said, "You're quite the traveler, little one, two months old and two countries. Aren't you something!" I squeezed him against me as we prepared to enter yet another.

We noticed quite a commotion ahead as we were approaching the Austrian border. There was definitely something out of the ordinary going on just ahead, but exactly what it was, we could not determine. We were motioned to pull over to the side of the road, along with many other cars parked haphazardly in the vicinity of the checkpoint, and strained our necks to see what was going on. It appeared to be mass confusion. Roadblocks were set up; many civilians milling around, talking excitedly; police or government officials directing traffic, barking instructions, making frantic gestures, indicating which cars should go where. It was obvious that there was more going on here than just the ordinary checking of credentials to permit the passing of one country into the other. Soon, two uniformed officials came over to the window on Johnny's side of the car and began speaking to him in what we assumed was German. It was definitely not French; of that, I was certain.

We could not decipher what the man was saying. Johnny was holding up our passports and other credentials. The man looked at these rather hurriedly but quickly began motioning and talking rapidly to us again. Seeing our questioning looks, he motioned another guard over to the car, and this one began talking to us. He was no more understandable than the first. We were all becoming quite frustrated; Johnny, at our inability to communicate, was anxious to move on as he knew this was the road that we must take to get to Innsbruck. The man too became frustrated at our inability to comprehend and relentlessly motioned us on.

"Bon chance," I thought I heard one say as we pulled back into the road and went on to drive around the barricade.

"Johnny, I could have sworn I heard the guard say, 'Good luck' in French as we pulled off. That was a nice thing to say, wasn't it?"

It was apparent to us in about five minutes, as we were climbing the mountain, why we had been wished good luck. We needed every bit of luck we could get and everyone else's too. As we came around a curve, we saw, to our astonishment, an assemblage of assorted vehicles coming directly at us, showing no regard for which side of the road they were on. Johnny jerked the car to the right, causing Terry's car bed to slide to the other side of the seat.

"Get in the back, Brenda. Quick!"

I tried to climb over the car seat and, at the same time, not lose my balance and fall on Johnny.

"You and Terry get in the back floorboard. Quick, hurry, hurry."

"What's happening, Johnny? What is it?"

He could not answer me for trying to maintain control of the car and avoid the oncoming vehicles. I quickly got Terry out of the car bed; and just as I was getting him out, I spotted, of all things, a motorcycle with a side seat, flying right past us.

"He barely missed us, Johnny. My gosh, what's happening?" I yelled, now terrified. "They're on the wrong side and flying too."

Johnny was perspiring by now and gripping the steering wheel so hard that his knuckles were white.

"Pray, honey, pray. They're racing for crying out loud, and we're the guinea pigs!"

I now had Terry in my arms underneath me as I crouched down behind the driver's side in the back floorboard.

"Can we pull over, Johnny? Can you get to the side?"

"No way. There are no sides. Don't look, honey. Just hold on, hold on tight. We've got no choice but to keep on going!"

As we made our way to the top of the mountain, the bulk of the traffic had passed, and Johnny said he was only seeing an occasional car or motorcycle.

"You can get up now," he said as he wiped his brow. "Are you and the baby all right?"

Terry, by this time, was screaming his head off but only because he had been wakened from his sleep and slung around in the car some; he was fine, though.

"Yeah, there's a place just ahead. We can pull over and survey the damage!"

By the time Johnny got the car stopped, he was furious.

"I can't believe anyone would put us in such a position as that – I can't believe it! They could have killed us!"

"What was it, Johnny? What happened?"

"Some kind of a darn road race is what it looked like. They were all flying down the mountain, heading toward those barricades we went around. That must have been the finish line."

"They did try to stop us, honey. That must have been what they were trying to tell us. We just couldn't understand. We're all three fine now, it's all right. Besides, it'll be something we can tell our grandchildren, that's for sure!"

THE QUILT

We spent the night in Innsbruck at a small bed and breakfast. In addition to the magnificent scenery, the thing that inspired me most was the feather-stuffed quilts on the bed.

"Johnny, isn't this heavenly! Lie down, honey. It's wonderful!"

"If you could only see yourself, Brenda, spread-eagled on that bed. You are so funny!" Johnny laughed.

"Come on. It's the softest, fluffiest thing imaginable. It's like being on a cloud," I urged. "You just sink in it."

It wasn't long until Johnny and I both were on the big bed, enjoying an indulgence we had never experienced before: a quilt stuffed with feathers. The pillows were fluffy and soft too. Compared to the bolster-type rolls the French used for pillows, this was indeed a luxury to which we had not experienced in the hotels of France.

"Put Terry on here, lay him on it, and see what he does!" I cried.

Soon, Terry was lying in the middle of the bed surrounded by mounds of fluffy quilt. He all but disappeared. We got him out immediately, for he could have actually smothered.

"Johnny, promise me when we get home that someday we'll have one of these quilts, please!"

"Brenda, honey, if that's all it takes to make you happy, I promise you'll have one. Somewhere we'll find a quilt of goose down." Then we clutched each other tightly and sunk even deeper into the voluptuous quilt.

#####

GERMANY

Johnny and I were eagerly anticipating our arrival in Garmisch. We had heard so much about this marvelous tourist area nestled in the Wetterstein Mountain range in the Bavarian Alps. The fame of this storybooklike place, we had been told, was due to the establishment of the Armed Forces Recreation Area in 1945. Johnny had been advised, before we left on our trip, that this would be an ideal place for us to spend some time before seeing our friends in Nuremburg.

"Johnny, look. Look ahead. The cows are in the street!" I cried.

"That explains the slowdown in traffic. I think this must be the usual thing; no one seems surprised or annoyed."

"They're even on the sidewalks," I exclaimed, amused at this strange sight.

The cows were sauntering along, making their way home after a day of grazing. They did provide us an opportunity for a closer view of this enchanting town from our car. As we were in no hurry and had nowhere to be at a certain time, we took advantage of this impromptu car "tour" of sorts. We were both looking from one side of the street to the other, trying to absorb as much as possible. The town was completely surrounded by mountains. We could see snowcapped peaks in every direction, rising high above and beyond the little shops, chalets, and hotels lining the streets.

The structures appeared to be made of concrete or stuccolike material with each one having elaborate wood-designed balconies overlooking the street. They all displayed multicolored flowers from wooden flower boxes underneath the windows or on ledges built on the bottom part of the balconies.

"Johnny, look at the artwork on that building. That's a painted window as sure as I live!"

We both looked at the building to the right with the beautiful and intricate artwork painted around the entrance and all of the windows. There was one window that was actually not a window at all but had been carefully painted to resemble one, curtains included!

We finally made our way to the Sheridan Plaza where we got settled in immediately. The hotel guests consisted of service men and their families from all over Europe, so we felt quite at home. It was a welcome relief to hear English being spoken by everyone we encountered.

The hotel clerk suggested that we see the ice show at the Cosa Carioca, a famous nightclub, when Johnny had inquired as to what was offered for entertainment. As baby-sitters were provided by the hotel, we were soon on our way to the show. The ice review was spectacular! We were enthralled with the figure skating, the gorgeous costumes, and the overall superb performance of each skater.

"I'm exhausted, Brenda. What about you?" Johnny asked after paying the baby-sitter and closing the door behind her.

"I'm ready for bed, but I loved that show, did you?"

"I'm not really into that ice stuff, but I thought it was great!"

"They really go all out for the service people here, don't they?" I said, more a statement than a question.

"It's a fantastic place to be. I'm glad I asked around before we made this trip. It would have been a shame to have missed this."

"Just think, as eager as we are to get home and show off Terry, I'm grateful people kept encouraging us to travel, even those from home."

Johnny got quiet when I mentioned home and said no more. I was aware the word "home" had conjured up memories of his father. My heart ached for him. As time drew closer to going home, I knew that, deep inside, Johnny had mixed emotions. As long as we were this far away, he had not really had to deal with the reality of his father's death. He could pretend things were as they were before we left, and upon our return, his father would be there; he could not imagine it any other way. I know I could not if our positions were reversed.

As we got into bed, in one of the most American-like atmospheres we had experienced in over a year, I thought about that goose-down quilt in the little inn we had spent the night before and how comfortable it had been. "I'll put that in the suggestion box," I thought. "To make this place completely perfect, furnish goose-down quilts for every room."

We spent several days in this charming area in the Bavarian Alps. We rented a baby carriage from the hotel and walked aimlessly along the streets, browsing in the shops, which had such tempting items. We wanted a sample of everything, which, obviously, we could not.

There were wood carvings of everything imaginable: music boxes, cuckoo and four-hundred day clocks, lederhosen, dirndl, and beer steins of all kinds. There were porcelain figurines, dinnerware, and wax art candles, which were unbelievably detailed.

We decided that Johnny must have the Bavarian green hat, symbol of the Bavarian Alps. Duck would get a kick out of that, we agreed, when Johnny arrived wearing that.

We got Terry a pair of lederhosen. He was too little to wear them now but could wear them later when he was big enough. They would never wear out and did not have to be washed. They were perfect for little boys, we were told. We got him the entire outfit: handmade socks, decorated suspenders, little coat, and hat. This would be his memento of the area and, hopefully, something he would have for years to come. We bought several beer steins for souvenirs, and I just had to have one of the fancy pipes for my father. That would make the perfect Christmas present for him.

On Thursday, Johnny and I left Terry at the hotel with a baby-sitter in order that we might take the all-day Zugspitze tour. We were told, just as we had been about Versailles Palace, that this was a must while we were in Garmisch. The tour started out by bus from Garmisch and crossed the Austrian border to Obermoos, Austria. Here, we took the cable-car ride to the Austrian Zugspitze hotel where we took a short walk through a tunnel, which came out at the Schneefernerhaus, the Bavarian hotel, highest in Germany.

Looking at the magnificent views of the mountains and the Zugspitze area gave me the same sense of exhilaration that I felt when in the Smoky Mountains of North Carolina. I always felt closer to God when in the mountains, and here, I experienced the same feeling as I looked out over his tremendous handiwork. It was breathtaking! Katherine Lee Bates must have felt the same way as she phrased the words of "America the Beautiful."

I took a deep breath of the cool fresh air and pushed my hands deeper into my coat pocket. It was, actually, freezing cold. We were fortunate, indeed, that we were prepared for the cold, even though it was early September.

By the time Johnny and I got back to the hotel, we knew it had been a day that we would never forget. Terry had been an angel, the baby-sitter informed us, which did not surprise us at all. He was sleeping soundly in the crib provided by the hotel.

"I don't think he's missed us at all, Johnny. What do you think?"

"He has, can't you tell? Just look how he's sleeping."

"What do you mean how he's sleeping?"

"He's worn-out, probably from crying so hard he's missed us so much."

"Oh, Johnny, you're a mess" as I flipped him with a towel.

This provoking action precipitated a game of sorts, Johnny chasing me around the room, pretending to be angry. In a playful mood, he caught me as I was trying to use Terry and his crib for cover.

"Don't wake Terry up!" I warned while laughing. "We'll never get to bed if he wakes up!"

"And what would be wrong with that?" Johnny responded as he grabbed me and held me tightly against his side. "I've missed him today; let's get him up!"

And we did just that. We woke Terry so that we could play with him and tell him about our day. It was after midnight before the three of us settled down, Terry lying between us in the double bed, both mine and Johnny's arms around him.

####

GERMANY

We arrived in Furth, Nuremburg on Friday, September 11. How odd it seemed to me to be in the country that had invaded and overtaken our adopted France and had posed such a threat to the entire world. I even felt a twinge of guilt for being in a country that had instilled such fear throughout the world such a short time ago. These thoughts had been running through my mind ever since we had crossed the German border.

We had marveled at the neat little farmhouses with the barns built as a part of the house as we traveled through the countryside. The animals may have been very close to the family living quarters, but the houses appeared neat and clean as could be. We learned later that this provided extra warmth for the families during the winter months.

What a marvelous reunion it was when we pulled in to the apartment complex in which Duck and Mary Alma lived. They were eagerly awaiting our arrival and greeted us with hugs and kisses. We all agreed it had to be the next best thing to being at home, seeing and being with friends from the same hometown. The four of us laughed, talked, and reminisced until the wee hours of the morning. Duck and Johnny had been such good friends at home that they had actually joined the army on the "buddy system."

"So much for the buddy system," Duck laughed heartily and slapped his knee as his cigar hung precariously from his mouth. "You in France and me in Germany!"

"Yes, but just look, Duck," Mary Alma smiled broadly and said, "look who your buddies are now, Brenda and me!"

"And we sure wouldn't have had a little Cindy and Terry around if you and I had remained buddies," Johnny quipped to Duck.

"These are the two best results I can think of for the two of you being separated," I said. "Who knows? Maybe little Cindy and little Terry will be buddies someday back home," and we all laughed.

Mary Alma and I behaved as if we had been the closest of friends at home. We developed an instant comradery and talked incessantly of mutual friends, families, our life in the service, and, of course, our babies.

Cindy, Duck and Mary Alma's baby, was three and a half months older than Terry. We joked about our little German girl and our little Frenchman.

I was amazed at the contrast in Duck and Mary Alma's life here in Germany and that of ours in France. She could not believe I had not talked on a telephone for over a year. The army required that every service family in the Furth Finance Disbursing Center have a telephone. She even had diaper service! I told her we were living like pioneers compared to them. We laughed good-naturedly when I described the type of "commode" we had and laughed even harder when I told her we felt lucky to have that. I was almost embarrassed to tell her we had an outdoor "privy" for eight months. It had really not bothered me, I went on to say. I had looked at everything as a kind of adventure, a test of some kind. It was temporary and that kept us going, a real challenge. There was no television, no hot water, and no washing machine, except for my little portable machine. "Where do you take a bath, Brenda?" Mary Alma inquired. I giggled when I told her I did not take baths; that was one of the things I was looking forward to most when I got home.

"Yes, I've been bathing from a pan now for about the past two months. We gain something and give up something every time we move," I said. "That's the first thing I intend to do when I get home." I continued, "Soak in hot bubble bath until I shrivel up."

"You've had it harder than we have, Brenda, I declare. I don't know how you've managed."

"You would do it too, Mary Alma. You would manage; it hasn't been that hard – honest."

We made a fuss over each other's children. They were both adorable, we were quick to say. Duck and Mary Alma would hold and make over Terry, and Johnny and I would do the same to Cindy. Mary Alma was so impressed that Terry slept through the night and drank eight ounces of milk when given a substitute bottle. I was amazed at how much Cindy looked like Duck; the resemblance was uncanny. Her little cheeks were so full and rosy that she was irresistible.

#####

A Tender Moment

The four of us were amused at the stares we drew from the German citizenry as Johnny carried Terry and Duck carried Cindy in their arms. Duck and Mary Alma explained that German men simply did not hold or make over their babies in public. The German women may have been a little envious that our husbands were so attentive to their offspring, and the German men may have thought they were jeopardizing their manhood.

The six of us went to Nuremburg to a place called Soldiers Field. Mary Alma and Duck told us that this was where Hitler had reviewed his troops. It reminded me of a huge football stadium. Mary Alma and I had Johnny take our pictures as we stood where supposedly Hitler had. It was an eerie feeling standing there, thinking perhaps that I may be standing exactly on the same spot that Hitler had once been. It gave me an uncanny feeling, for this man, in my mind, epitomized evil.

"How did a person like him rise to such power?" I pondered. "Why had the German people been so mesmerized by him?" I had read that he was an excellent orator and could have an audience of thousands in the palm of his hand after he spoke to them. "But how did he become so vicious and cruel? He had to have had a mother and a father that loved him at some time in his life. What happened?"

Mary Alma pointed out the huge columns Hitler had ordered built, symbolizing each country he had conquered. It gave me cold chills when she pointed out the half-finished column representing the United States.

Just being in this place brought to mind a poignant memory from my childhood that I had not thought about for years. I was a little girl of five, a few months from being six years old and in the United States, but, yet, had an encounter with a German prisoner of war. It was an unbelievable incident but, indeed, had occurred.

My grandmother was working as a maid in a motel in the western part of Tennessee, near her home of Paris, during the summer of 1944. In order for my mother and I to visit her, it was necessary for us to share Ma Maw's quarters in the motel.

"Ma Maw," as I fondly called my grandmother, was fending for herself at the time as she had been doing since my grandfather had left her many years before. She had worked in beauty shops, kept children, and nursed the elderly in order to support herself and two little girls: my mother and her younger sister. Now, she had taken a job in a special place indeed, a German prisoner-of-war camp in the state of Tennessee. These camps were not widely made known to the public for fear of creating anxiety among the population. Actually, there was no danger, as my mother had explained to me in later years, for the German prisoners, for the most part, were content to wait the war out. They were clothed, fed, and treated well. Many of them felt fortunate to be where they were – in prison – rather than fighting. As to whether this was true or not, or my mother was trying to soothe my concerns about the prisoners, I do not know.

She and I had been visiting my grandmother at this place for several weeks when one of the American officers approached my grandmother with an unusual request.

"We have a German officer among the prisoners who is being transferred from this camp today. He has asked if he may speak to your little granddaughter before he leaves."

"Why? Why would he want to see my granddaughter? No, there is no way I could allow that," my grandmother emphatically replied, "and how does he know her anyway?"

"Well, Mrs. Dolson, with all respect, it seems she had been entertaining, if you'll excuse the word, the prisoners every afternoon when they are in the exercise yard."

"My lord, sir, you must be mistaken, and what in the world do you mean by 'entertain,' anyway? She's only five years old!"

"Ma'am, she's been jumping rope up and down the length of the fence, skipping and so on. You know, whatever little girls do to entertain themselves. The prisoners have been watching her for days; they look forward to seeing her."

"Colonel, I find this beyond belief, and my answer is still no. I'm sorry."

"Let me explain, Mrs. Dolson, please. Maybe the word 'entertain' is a bad choice of words. This officer has been a model prisoner, speaks halting English, and, in honesty, has all but pleaded to see her. We'll be right there with her. I can promise you there is no danger."

In the end, it was my mother who made the decision to let me meet the German prisoner. The American officer had explained to her that the men had not seen their girlfriends, wives, or, possibly, children in years. They had loved watching the little curly-haired blonde girl in her little dresses and starched white pinafores, playing alongside the fence.

When my mother had asked me if I was aware the "men" were watching me, I had immediately responded that I was.

"I felt sorry for those men, Mother. They were locked up behind that old fence, so I danced for them, and they liked it too!" I replied quite honestly.

The meeting took place behind the open-ended back of an army truck. I was escorted by several soldiers out to the truck, which was preparing to depart, as my mother and grandmother looked anxiously from a distance.

With all the humbleness and sincerity a human being could possible exhibit, the German officer knelt on the ground so that he would be closer to me. Trustingly and without hesitation, I walked right into his arms, for I knew he wanted to tell me something. With tears in his eyes, he whispered to me so that none of the others could hear, his rough, calloused hand tenderly touching my arm, "I left a little girl about your age at home when I went to fight in the war. I do not know if she will be there when I get back or not." He paused, wiping perspiration from his brow, "Would you kiss me good-bye, please?" I nodded and was about to kiss him right then when he put his hand up and gently wiped his cheek clean with a handkerchief and indicated that, now, I could kiss him on the spot he had just wiped.

I kissed him on the cheek and told him good-bye, and with that, he climbed up into the army truck and waved a fond good-bye. I often wondered if he had found his little girl when he returned to Germany.

My grandmother and mother told me years later that many of the other German prisoners, and even some of the American guards who witnessed this tender scene, were wiping their eyes as the truck pulled off.

At that moment, Johnny asked us if Mary Alma or I would take a picture of him and Duck, each holding the other's baby.

"Of course," Mary Alma responded. "They'll love that back home."

####

PARTY DOLL

That night, we attended a carnival in Furth. It was a crisp fall night with the aroma of bagels baking, hot sausages sizzling on the grills, and potatoes frying in the air. The crowd was in a festive mood, obviously, and ready for a night of fun. We heard the strains of the oompah band floating across the fairway as we approached the massive tent where it was located, the deep bass practically shaking the ground.

"Brenda," Mary Alma advised, "you've probably never seen anything like this, so be prepared. The Germans really enjoy themselves!"

I could hardly wait to get inside and begin having fun with them! Music, revelry, dancing, and drinking – I had never seen so much of all four going on in one place. We had heard so much about the famous German beer I felt we should at least taste it. "It would be a shame to be in Germany and not taste the beer," I told myself.

We managed to squeeze through the massive crowd of merrymakers and found seats along one of the many tables surrounding the band. It was in the center of the crowd high above on a bandstand. The members were wearing the native costumes, I assumed, of the area. Pitchers of beer donned every table. People were drinking and singing, swaying back and forth in time to the music and, in general, having a grand time.

"They can get pretty boisterous, Johnny," Duck warned, "but I've never seen people have as good a time anywhere."

"Let's try the beer," I eagerly requested. I could barely tolerate the wine in France, but with the reputation Germans had for their beer, I knew it must be really special.

"We don't drink it, honey; it's powerful, but if you want to try, you can. We'll get some for you and Johnny."

"Brenda, I'm not drinking that stuff, but if you want to try it, go ahead." Johnny said.

An hour or so later, I was standing up on one of the benches, on which we had been sitting alongside some other Germans, arm in arm, swaying back and forth to the most exhilarating music I had ever heard.

"This is more fun than the stroll!" I yelled down to Mary Alma who was looking up at me incredulously.

"I love the way they say no. 'Nine, nine' – isn't that just the cutest thing?" I said as Johnny was helping me down from the bench.

Duck was laughing and saying at the same time, "She's only had a stein. That stuff is potent, I tell you!"

"Mary Alma, where are we going next?" I asked while feeling slightly dizzy.

"I think we're going home. You've had a good time, haven't you?"

"Gosh, yes, it's been great!"

The next morning, when Mary Alma asked me teasingly what it felt like to be a party doll, I told her that I believed I would stick with the French and their wine. I could not bear to drink enough wine to make me cross-eyed, much less dance on a bench.

We had all enjoyed one another's company so much that Duck and Mary Alma insisted we stay longer. Duck would take Monday off, and we would all be together at least one more day. I recalled one of Benjamin Franklin's sayings about visitors and fish smelling after three days but knew that our host and hostess were sincere in their invitation to stay longer. We were having the time of our lives. If we had missed talking about or asking about one single person in our little town back home, we could not think of them. Duck and Johnny were enjoying each other's company, and Mary Alma and I loved talking about home and our babies.

It was a tearful good-bye as we left our friends. Johnny and Duck had always been close, and now, I felt a special bond to Mary Alma. We had shared so many feelings with each other in the past five days I knew we would always remember this special time together. We, all four, made repeated promises of getting together when we got back home.

####

Home Again

While touring the famous Rhine River, I could not help but think that once we got home, we would be back in our own country – France. How odd it seemed to think of France as "our" country, but that is how I felt now, standing there, looking over the railings lining the ferry. Someone had said before I left the States that to spend a year in France would be the equivalent of a year in college. I had not understood what that statement meant at the time, but now, I thought I did. The past two weeks had certainly brought us new and wonderful sights of which we had never dreamed. We had been exposed to the people of Switzerland, Austria, and Germany. True, we only covered small portions of the countries, but it had awakened a desire to see and learn more about other people throughout the world.

"Brenda, what are you smiling about, looking out at that water?" Johnny asked while pressing nearer to me, holding Terry protectively in his arms.

"I was just thinking how I want to go to many more places and see a lot more things just as soon as I can."

"We will, sweetheart, we will," Johnny said softly. "We have a lifetime ahead of us; we'll see all kinds of things."

"But first, you've got to find a job when we get back home, hon, before we can do anything. "Johnny, would you consider staying in the army? I think I would love it."

"Not a chance. I want to be my own person and do things my own way. I want Terry to have a stable life, not moving around every couple of years," Johnny responded.

"It could be an advantage, being in the army. Think of all the places we could live and all the things we could see."

"Yeah, how would you like living in Alaska? You might not think it was such an advantage then," Johnny quipped.

"You're probably right about that, but you'll have to admit we've certainly made the best of adverse conditions in France."

Johnny, looking serious, said to me, "I would never have made it over here without you, darling. I mean that with all my heart. You and Terry have made my life complete. I can't imagine life anywhere without the two of you."

"Well, Johnny Stroupe, if you weren't holding Terry and we weren't in front of all these people, I'd kiss you to death!"

"Hey, I'll hold you to that tonight!" Johnny challenged in a playful tone.

The boat's motors seemed to be gearing down, signaling that we were preparing to dock. We made our way, along with the other passengers, to the car, anxious now to get home as our trip was coming to an end.

####

SIRENS WAILING

Our return trip to Orleans brought exciting news. Johnny had received notice that his rotation date would be January 18. This meant that he would be discharged from the army and leaving for home in less than four months!

Our letters were now filled with plans for the future and questions as well. We knew we wanted to stay in or near our little hometown of Cherryville, if that were possible, but all would depend upon Johnny finding employment. There were questions as to where we would stay upon our immediate return and what kind of job Johnny would find. We were also considering the possibility of Johnny continuing his education while, perhaps, I worked. This would require a baby-sitter.

My father was trying his best to offer advice and act as a consultant of sorts, which we welcomed. It was apparent that he felt a double sense of responsibility now that Johnny's father, Garland, was gone and strived to give us sound counseling.

My mother, on the other hand, was concerned with one thing: Rosenthal china. She had been advising me for months that we should purchase our china while in Europe. It was much cheaper, she had written, and it was absolutely necessary that I pick out a pattern and get it now before I come home. Not knowing anything whatsoever about china, and dishes being one of the least of my concerns, I diligently, however, set about trying to purchase this particular brand of china. It seemed terribly important to Mother, and she did know a great deal about these matters. Johnny was easily convinced, after I discussed it with him, that china was a top priority in setting up housekeeping in the United States.

She and I then passed letters back and forth across the ocean concerning china patterns. I would send Mother the brochures and prices, and she, in turn, would give me her opinion.

In spite of our growing interest and energies toward leaving the secure life of the service and going home, our life continued, as usual, in the little apartment above the streets of Orleans.

I was an ardent listener of Arthur Godfrey every morning at nine o'clock. Terry and I listened to his program regularly while I fed Terry oatmeal mixed with fruit. He loved that combination and had an excellent appetite.

I would often perform for Terry, as he was my sole companion for the most part, throughout the day. I would dance around in the kitchen while beating rhythms on a pot with a spoon. He would grin broadly and wave his little arms in the air and kick his legs, which only egged me on. He and I both especially loved "Let the Good Times Roll," and I would play it over and over again on the record player and dance with him in my arms. We were having one of these "playful" moments one morning after Johnny had left for work when a frightening thing happened.

After feeding and playing with Terry, I had dressed him up in one of the cute outfits that had been given to us at the baby shower. I put him on little socks and shoes, brushed his hair, and sat back to admire him. Then I got the idea to sit him on one of the dining-room chairs. I wanted to see how he would look all dressed up with the chair's back providing a fancy background. Terry had recently begun trying to sit up on his own. He would sit up, lean over, and, eventually, fall forward, but he was learning. I placed him on the chair and, without thinking, stepped back to look at my precious little boy. At that precise moment, as I took my hands from Terry and moved backward, he suddenly lurched sideways off the chair, headfirst onto the hard marble floor below. He screamed vehemently. I was horrified!

"What have I done? What have I done?" my mind was screaming. I picked him up and completely panicked. I needed help and quick. I rushed to the window, flung open the shutters, and yelled down into the street below what I thought to be the word for "help" in French. I was only met with puzzled stares from the people on the street below. Seeing I was not going to get any help that way, I rushed down the flight of steps with Terry in my arms, still howling at the top of his lungs, and opened the main door to the streets. I ran to a nearby French beauty shop and went bursting in, yelling, "Telephono, telephono." The people in their plastic capes and half-done hairdos looked at me in startled amazement. It did not occur to me until days later what a shock that must have been, a half-crazed American woman storming into a French beauty shop with her baby screaming at the top of his lungs and her, obviously upset, trying to say, "Telephone."

A concerned male beautician came to my aid immediately and asked whom he could call for me. Not knowing Johnny's number, as I had never had a phone, I answered, "The MPs. Call the MPs, and please hurry; my baby's hurt!" The MPs were there in minutes as we were not far from the base, their sirens screaming. They put us in the car immediately and went speeding toward the hospital. The sirens only made Terry cry louder, which convinced me he was dying.

"What happened, lady? What happened to the baby? What's wrong?" the MP who was in the passenger seat asked as the other one was driving like crazy to get through the traffic and down the narrow streets.

"He fell on his head!" I heard myself saying. "Oh my god," I thought, "that sounds horrible" as I was trying to console Terry and, at the same time, praying he was all right.

"How, lady, how did he do that?"

"You see, I sat him in a chair to look at him – oh lord, you'd never understand. I can't explain it. Just hurry, please."

The MP looked at me quite puzzled, and it was then it occurred to me what he might be thinking.

"It was an accident; it was my fault, but I didn't mean for him to fall," I tried to explain hysterically.

"Ma'am, I know that. Just calm down. We'll be there in a minute – can you tell me how to get in touch with your husband?"

Later on, when I was assured that Terry was perfectly all right and Johnny was en route to the hospital, the wise and kind doctor consoled me by saying that I was in far worse shape than the baby.

"These things happen to babies all the time," he said, "even when parents are right beside them. With this being a boy, you're going to see more than this little bump in the months ahead."

"I feel horrible, just horrible about the whole thing. I couldn't bear to think I had caused him to be hurt."

"You didn't, Mrs. Stroupe, you didn't. You've shown you're a loving, caring mother by being where you are right now. More than likely, he would have stopped crying a few minutes after he fell. When you became so alarmed, he became even more frightened."

"Thank you, thank you so much for your help and support, Doctor. This means more to me than you'll ever know."

"By the way, Mrs. Stroupe, what were you yelling out the window?"

"Apogee, apogee!" I answered.

The doctor's face broke into a huge grin. "Why, Mrs. Stroupe, you were yelling 'Acne, acne!'"

"Oh my gosh, no wonder they looked at me so funny!"

Johnny, quite shaken, picked the two of us up at the hospital and took us home.

Terry was cooing and smiling like nothing had happened, content as he could be.

"That doctor," I thought to myself, "reminded me of my father and what he might have said under similar circumstances, and somehow, I felt a little wiser for having had the experience."

REFLECTIONS

For my twentieth birthday, Johnny surprised me with a beautiful black leather jacket, a big box of chocolates, and two birthday cards, one from him and one from Terry. I began crying as we slow danced to "Happy, Happy Birthday, Baby" that Johnny had put on the record player. I cried not because of the sweet sentiments Johnny had written but largely because he had remembered to have a card for me from Terry. I was touched, my first birthday card from my son. Here, I was spending my second birthday in France. I thought of my birthday last year: the cake Alice's mother had made and decorated for me and how affected I had been by that act. I thought of our sweet little Simone and wondered how she was faring now that she was back home with her parents. I recalled the Higgins and Sue and Dee and how nice they had been to take us out again for my birthday. I smiled to myself, thinking how funny they thought it was that Johnny and I ate "banana" sandwiches; they had never heard of such a thing. I wondered how the Higgins and their boys were enjoying Fort Jackson, South Carolina.

"I bet they see plenty of people eating banana sandwiches in South Carolina."

I wrote my father, "Daddy, remember how, on my tenth birthday, I felt so grown up because I was on my tenth finger and you said, 'Brenda, you've still got your toes to go'? Well, here I am - on the tenth toe."

Sue and Dee gave us a nice present indeed, a night of baby-sitting. They would take care of Terry in order that we could go out "on the town." Since it had been awhile since we had seen Bridgie and Vince, as we now were living in the city, we thought it would be an excellent opportunity to ask them if they would like to go with us. Johnny made the arrangements from the office. They would be delighted, Vince had told Johnny, and they would love being with us and catching up on things again. It was decided that we would have dinner at a nice French restaurant in the heart of Orleans.

I stared unbelievably at the plate across the table from me: snails! Vince had ordered escargot! There were twelve snails, still in their shells, just sitting up on that plate, looking exactly as if they were ready to crawl off. It was sickening! Vince had to have special utensils in order to pull the snail out of its shell and eat it. I could hardly eat; in fact, neither could Bridgie. She told Vince she was not going to kiss him again until he had washed his mouth out with soap. I certainly could not blame her. Those would be my sentiments exactly if Johnny were to pull such a stunt. I was aware escargot was considered a delicacy here, but I found it a repulsive sight.

We caught up on the news of the others at the compound. They told us that Martine, Franswa, Renee, and Pierre still came and played with the American children, and Monsieur had even put up two swings for them. Bridgie knew we would enjoy hearing that.

I thought about the day, a little over a year ago, when I had discovered the four of them taking paper napkins from the trash can. Of all the many things I had to be thankful to God for, wadded-up paper napkins, which had attracted the children, was one of the things I was most thankful for. Who would have ever dreamed of the marvelous outcome those seemingly insignificant paper napkins would emit. How we cherished the children's friendship and that of their families.

"What would we ever have done without Mama?" I reflected, thinking about her encompassing motherly concern for us. She had, from a distance, "looked after" her surrogate American children quite well.

By the time we got back home, I was in a melancholy mood indeed. Sue and Dee would allow none of that, however, and immediately cleared the table for a game of canasta. We played cards until one o'clock in the morning.

####

PREPARATIONS

We began now in earnest taking orders from the folks back home concerning anything they would like us to buy for them at a good price while we were still in the service. We found ourselves with money orders from family members and friends to purchase such items as cameras, binoculars, cashmere sweaters, and jewelry. One relative had even requested that we try to get the famous Joy perfume of France. We found ourselves busy indeed, trying to purchase and send requested items home for others, as well as getting our own personal items sorted and assembled for mailing. We were trying to send ahead clothing and goods that we would not be needing for the next two months. We knew we would have to leave what little furniture we had for Terry behind. Those items would either be sold or divided among friends. There was nothing unusual at all for service families to leave goods for other families when being transferred to other bases. It was easier and simpler to purchase whatever one might need after they reached their new assignments.

Our families were gathering together the necessary items required for Terry from other relatives and friends. They already had the necessities, a crib, a high chair, and a play pen. They were having a good time, I knew, getting things together for their grandson.

As the military would be sending Johnny home, it was necessary that Terry and I come separately. Johnny was hoping I could get on a space available flight, which meant I could fly on a military flight, and it not cost anything. However, if this did not materialize, it would be necessary that we come on a commercial flight for which we would have to bear the cost. Either way, we knew I would be home at least a month before Johnny.

Daddy, therefore, was happily getting the basement in proper order for a temporary living quarters for us. He even told me he had painted the chest of drawers I had used as a child. I knew Daddy was in his dimension, piddling and fixing things up. Why, we could stay there as long as we wanted, he had written; he and mother would love to have the three of us for as long as we needed a place to stay. I knew he could not wait to get his hands on his grandson. If we thought Terry was spoiled now, it would be nothing compared to how spoiled he would be once we were home.

I was hoping too that Terry might help Johnny's mother, Naomi, fill the void in her life. "She'll see Garland in Terry," I thought. "He'll bring her so much joy, I know he will. He'll charm her, just as he has us, and make her laugh and smile and realize that life goes on."

Terry was growing and changing so almost before our eyes. He was now getting up on all fours – his hands and knees in a crawling position – and rocking back and forth. He made quite a racket in his crib doing just that, causing the crib to squeak and creak. We thought this was real cute until he woke up and started doing this in the middle of the night. I would hear this noise in the mornings, get out of bed, and ease myself to the door separating our room from his. It made no difference at what level I would try to peep around the doorframe to spy on him; he would invariably spot me every time and break out in a broad grin. I would then go straight to him, pick him up, and squeeze him tight.

"They're going to love you back home, little man. Your grandparents, aunts, uncles, and cousins are going to spoil you rotten." I kissed him on his cheek and thought about Garland. How sad it was that Garland would never get to see this precious little boy with his ready smile and winsome ways. "He knew, though," I comforted myself, "that Terry had been born, and we can thank God for that."

One night, Johnny kept Terry while Sue and I went to the movies to see *The Diary of Anne Frank*. I found the movie to be intriguing but upsetting. I had read the book and had been affected by it, but seeing the movie here in France made the story even more poignant. Passing the partially bombed cathedral, which had been damaged during the war, only heightened my senses of the devastation and destruction of lives that World War II had reeked. So many lives destroyed and so many innocent victims murdered in such atrocious ways. It gave me goose bumps to think what the end result may have been if Adolf Hitler had been successful in carrying out his plans for world domination. Thank God, it had ended when it did.

Johnny had a surprise for me when I got home. He had washed the diapers and mopped the floor! That was a wonderful surprise in itself, but Johnny said that was not the big one.

"What? What, Johnny? Tell me or I'll die of suspense," I pleaded.

"You'll never guess, so I may as well tell you. Come over here and rub your fingers on Terry's lower gums!"

I proceeded to do just that and squealed with delight when I felt a distinct hard bulge protruding through his gums: definitely enamel!

"A tooth, Terry has a tooth!"

"No, not just 'a' tooth," Johnny stated smugly, "but two teeth. Look again!"

Sure enough, Terry had two little teeth in the middle of his lower gums! Johnny was elated that he had made this amazing discovery when I was with Terry all the time and had not noticed them. I was really quite happy he had discovered them; he was so excited about it.

"Four months old and Terry has two teeth, discovered by his father," we proudly wrote in Terry's baby book.

#####

THANKSGIVING

Troy and Jack came to spend Thanksgiving Day with us. We welcomed their company. They adored Terry, always bringing him presents and making over him, and they always brought laughter and fun. The four of us, along with little Terry, thoroughly enjoyed being together. In fact, they were making tentative plans to take Johnny to Holland with them in January. I, of course, would be home by then. I thought this would be grand, for I knew Johnny would miss Terry and me dreadfully.

One of the extra benefits of Troy and Jack coming on Thanksgiving was that they insisted on preparing the meal as they had done before on occasions. Troy was a tall stout fellow who would don his big white bib apron and proceed to "take over" the kitchen. When I looked at him in there – so funny looking with his apron tied high above his generous waist, busily jangling pots and pans and pulling dishes out – I would smile to myself and think, "And those back home feel sorry for us, not having television here to watch. They just don't know what they're missing either!"

Troy and Jack had brought four steaks, two quarts of chocolate milk, two quarts of ice cream, two pies, potato chips, lettuce, and tomatoes.

"My gosh, guys," Johnny exclaimed, "you've got enough food to feed the Pilgrims and the Indians!" They had brought a monopoly board with them for after dinner entertainment. As it happened, Sue and Dee came by later in the afternoon, and the six of us played monopoly until late that night. Kenny amused himself with his miniature trucks and soldiers, and Terry either slept or watched us from his crib. We all agreed that it had been a wonderful Thanksgiving Day, and we were thankful, among many other things, that we had friends with whom we could share the holiday.

Planning Ahead

Excitement was mounting as definite plans were being made toward Terry and me going back to North Carolina. The space available flight had not worked out; therefore, I was to be flying home on a commercial one. As special Christmas package deals were being offered, we could actually purchase a round-trip ticket from Paris to New York cheaper than a one-way flight. This was what we had decided to do. The TWA airline agency had advised us to not cancel the return-trip ticket but simply not show up. Terry and I would be leaving Paris at nine o'clock Sunday night on December 20 and arriving in New York at 7:50 a.m. Mike and Jean, who were now married, were planning to meet me in New York. I could not wait to see the two of them and, at the same time, them to see Terry. "That's really something," I thought. "They saw me off sixteen months ago, and this time, when they meet me, there's two!"

Daddy had written and encouraged me to perhaps stay in New York a few days with friends of his in order that I may tour the big city.

"You may not have the chance again," he advised. "It would be an opportune time."

I wrote right back, "Who cares a flick about seeing New York when I can see all of you?"

There were some mixed emotions going on inside me now that I could not really understand. I shared these intimate feelings with my mother in a letter.

"As much as I'm dying to come home and as homesick as I am, I'm afraid. Isn't that silly? This is all I've dreamed and thought about for a whole year, and now that it's almost here, I'm anxious. I wonder about such things like will people still like me or if I'll seem different now. How will everyone look and how will the town look? I wonder. Where will my place be exactly? I'm not only a married woman but have a baby as well. I'm not the carefree, happy-go-lucky teenager that everyone so fondly bid farewell. Mother, do you understand?"

Not only did she understand she tried valiantly to convince me that everything was going to be just fine. In fact, Mrs. Smith, my social studies teacher from high school, had requested that I bring Terry to class one day and tell them about my experiences in France.

"You're kind of in demand, darling Some people from various clubs have even approached your father and me about you talking to their groups." Instead of reassuring me, this news only served to petrify me. Just the thought of speaking in front of a group of people made my stomach churn.

If that was not bad enough, my father had written an addition in mother's letter that there was a slight possibility a television crew might be on hand at the airport to film a Sun Drop commercial on my arrival. It seems he had contacted some Sun Drop officials about me having requested that they have me a bottle of Sun Drop ready at the airport. Sun Drop was my favorite drink, and I had not had one in sixteen months. My dear sister-in-law had even tried to send us some at one point, but when the post office learned glass bottles were involved, she was not allowed to send them.

"Oh my gosh," I thought, "instead of them helping, they're making matters worse. As though I did not have enough to worry about traveling with a baby all night, one layover in New York of six hours, and then a five-hour flight to Charlotte. I had been concerned about mine and Terry's appearance upon our arrival to meet family and friends. Now, I had this to think about too; it was just too much! Lord, Daddy, why not just call out the town band too while you're at it? If he thinks about it, he'd do it as sure as the world," I thought mournfully but could not help but grin a little at the thought.

#####

Saying Good-bye

Our Christmas presents for family and friends had been sent a month before I was to leave in order that the things would arrive before Christmas. The Rosenthal china was en route also; I considered giving it to my mother for Christmas but decided we could share it. I had finally decided on a definite modern pattern, with gray lids topping the accessory pieces and the same color bordering the plates. I hoped mother liked it. Johnny was to spend Christmas with Sue, Dee, and little Kenny. It made me feel better, knowing he would be seeing a little boy at Christmas getting his Santa Claus and all. I knew that would help, but it would not be easy. Nor would it be easy for me either, but I, at least, would be spending Christmas with family. Johnny was planning to move back into the barracks in January. He would be there just a little over two weeks when it would be his turn to come home.

Johnny and I had been so busy making arrangements and preparing to go home that we had not gotten back to the compound to tell everyone there good-bye. The day before I was to leave, we dressed Terry up, put his little blue bunting suit on him, and took off.

"Oh, Johnny, this makes me kind of sad" as we drove down the streets of Saint-Jean de Bray. We passed the little cafe in which I had embarrassed myself so. "Johnny had never been told anything about this incident, but I would tell him someday," I thought to myself. There was the school where I had watched the children at play through the fence. The little park where I had met Simone and Alice looked cold and deserted now here in December.

We created quite a stir once we got inside the compound gates. We went immediately to Bridgie and Vince's because of the cold. It was not long until Monsieur Roche was there, along with Correen and Roy. Colonel and Mrs. Tanner even came when Mark had run over to tell them we were here to say good-bye. They all made over Terry, which pleased us to no end, and told us how they wished they could be there to see our families when they saw Terry for the first time. They all commented about the fact that Terry was almost six months old. They could not believe it.

Monsieur went to his house and brought back one of his best bottles of wine. Then everyone toasted us and wished us good luck in our new life back in the States. I could have sworn I saw a tear in Monsieur's eye but could not be certain. We thanked all of them profusely for all the help they had given us during the smoke incident and the love and concern they had shown us during the death of Johnny's father. Then we told them we must be getting on so that we could see Mama and Papa and Madam Cassier. We all promised we would write and keep in touch. Monsieur fondly kissed Terry on both cheeks.

Telling Mama and Papa and Martine good-bye was even harder than bidding our American friends good-bye. We knew, as Mama and Papa did, they had been an important part of our lives here in France. They had been the surrogate parents for us and Martine the little sister for both Johnny and I that we had left at home.

Johnny gave Mama our going-away present: a dozen two-pound bags of kernels of popcorn. This provided a chuckle for everyone, and Mama proceeded to pantomime the first time she popped the corn without the lid. I told Papa to tell her to be sure to put the lid on when she popped the corn from now on. Papa interpreted, and Mama proceeded to speak rapidly in French and nodding that she understood. We gave Martine a porcelain doll dressed in a United States' red, white, and blue dress. For Papa, we had a carton of cigarettes. We knew he would like this as much as anything.

Again, we made promises of writing and keeping in touch while hugging and kissing. Then Mama had a surprise. She had crocheted Terry a little sweater and cap. Tears filled my eyes as she brought out the beautifully crocheted little blue sweater and cap. I promised her that he would wear them on the trip home.

Madam Cassier was not at home.

"She's probably at her friend's, watching television," I told Johnny, so we left her a farewell note and a picture of Terry.

"You know, Johnny, the shutter's being closed and the street's being so desolate; don't bother my anymore."

"Why is that, hon?"

"Because we know some of the people behind then now," I said, giving a little shrug of my shoulders while holding Terry on my lap.

#####

Going Home

A boy from Johnny's office, who was going home for Christmas, accompanied us to Orly Field in Paris on that cold, gray December evening to catch our plane.

Dennis, the boy who was going home on a thirty-day leave, had assured Johnny he would help me any way he could with Terry. He would be by my side, he said, as soon as we landed in Iceland to refuel and again in New York to help me get through customs. I was truly grateful for this added support as I was growing more and more uneasy about not only leaving Johnny but making this long trip by myself. The time passed too quickly once we arrived at the airport, and I was trying to say all the things to Johnny I wanted to say, and before I knew it, our flight was being called to board.

Pete grabbed me and hugged me tight. "I'm going to miss you, girl. I'm really going to miss you."

"Take care of Johnny for me, Pete. Just take care of him, please."

"Hey, I did before you got here, didn't I?" He then squeezed Terry and said to Dennis, "We're countin' on you, buddy, to look after these two."

Dennis gave the thumbs-up sign and winked, "You betcha. I gotta work with you two when I get back."

They both stepped aside so that Johnny and I could speak privately as the passengers were beginning to board.

"Have you got everything, honey, your tickets ready and all?"

"Yes, they're right here. I have them right here."

"I'll see you in a month, honey, and then we'll have a new beginning, a new life together back home," Johnny whispered. "Take care of my baby till I get there."

"You know I will, Johnny. You have a happy Christmas and remember how much we'll be thinking of you and love you," I said as the line of people began moving forward toward the gates, separating passengers from ones coming to see them off.

Then suddenly, I had to move on. We kissed quickly, and I yelled to Johnny as I was going through the gate, "Don't forget to get Kenny a present!" and Johnny and Pete were out of sight.

True to his word, Dennis was right by my side as we boarded the plane. He saw that I was settled in with Terry, and then he went to find his seat.

I could hear the roar of the motors as they began to prepare for the takeoff, and I felt that same sense of exhilaration I had felt when I flew for the first time. We began taxiing down the runway; the plane was gaining speed, and suddenly, we lifted, lifted up into the sky. I knew that somewhere down below Pete and Johnny were watching as we disappeared into the clouds.

I started crying. I realized I was not crying because I was leaving Johnny. I was crying because I was leaving a part of me behind too. It was true. A part of my heart and soul would forever remain in France. How could it not? I had lived my first year and a half of marriage here, I had become a mother here, and we had mourned the death of a loved one here. Yes, I was crying. Why shouldn't I?

Johnny and I had grown up a lot in the past sixteen months. We were leaving more than memories in France; we were leaving our innocence.

The pilot announced over the speaker, "Ladies and gentlemen, fasten your seat belts securely, and I will give you an additional treat to your flight. Paris, the city of lights, is attired for Christmas. I will dip the wings slightly as we circle the city for your pleasure."

With that, the plane dipped so that I could plainly see the lights of Paris below. An awesome quietness spread throughout the entire plane. "I'll Remember (In the Still of the Night)" tune crossed my mind, for I knew I would remember this moment the rest of my life as the plane leveled off and headed west. What a perfect way to say good-bye.

I was on my way again, but on my way to what? I did not know and I did not care, for I now not only had Johnny but Terry as well. The three of us, together, could face whatever might lie before us.

I looked down into my baby's sweet little blue eyes, looking up at me with all the trust in the world. I drew him closer to me, leaned my head over, and whispered softly in his ear, "We're going home, darling, we're going home!"

THE END

Printed in the United States
24348LVS00001B/7-63